SHADES OF MURDER

A SEEING COLORS MYSTERY BOOK 1

J. A. WHITING

To hear about new books and book sales, please sign up for my mailing list at:

www.jawhitingbooks.com

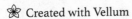 Created with Vellum

For my family with love

1

N ell Finley stood at the big windows in the white-walled backroom-studio of her shop looking out over the Bluewater Cove neighborhood and at the ocean beyond. Dark clouds had gathered, low and thick, and a bolt of lightning flashed between them.

Beads of sweat formed on Nell's forehead and her body turned cold.

"It's only a quick thunderstorm. It will be over in five minutes." Nell's sister, Violet, called to her from the front of the store.

Nell didn't answer. She closed her eyes and took in slow, deep breaths, but the not-unexpected wave of anxiety started in her feet, climbed up over her legs, wrapped around her torso, and rattled in her head.

Iris, the light brown, medium-sized, Lab-Poodle mix stared up at the young woman and anxiously tapped her tail on the floor.

Whirling, Nell hurried towards the staircase that led to the finished basement of the large, antique Cape-style home where the sisters kept their shop in two of the rooms facing Main Street and lived in the rest of the house.

"Wait." Violet came into the studio, concern showing in her green eyes. "I'll stay with you in here. Let's sit next to each other until it passes."

"I'll be okay. I have to go down to the basement." Nell disappeared down the stairs with Iris running after her, and when she reached the lower level, she rushed to the rocking chair, sat down and wrapped a blanket over her shoulders, closed her eyes, and whispered to herself, over and over while patting the dog's head ... *it will be over in minutes. I'll be all right. Nothing's going to happen.*

Ten months ago, Nell and Violet's mother passed away in the family home in central Massachusetts. Nell had gone to the house to start cleaning it out and, during a break, she sat at the kitchen table eating the lunch she'd brought along with her.

The day was hot and humid and the air was oddly still. When she'd taken a few trash bags to the garage, Nell noticed the strange yellow-green of the overcast sky.

Sitting at the table, she was about to take a bite of her sandwich when the sound of a train could be heard off in the distance. Even though there were no train tracks nearby, the rumble grew to a roar and then the heavens opened and rain fell like a tidal wave over the house.

Nell's heart had pounded like a jackhammer and she stood up so fast her chair slid back three feet from the table.

Standing aghast as uprooted trees flew past the kitchen window, she took off for the cellar when the glass in the living room bay window shattered and blew out.

Crouching in a basement corner as the storm roared over the family home, the building began to shake and groan, and twenty seconds later, the house lifted from its foundation and blasted away with the tornado leaving Nell in the dark, open cellar hole, the wind pummeling her, and the rain lashing down on her body.

The F-4 tornado killed twenty-seven people that day as it tore through five small towns before dissipating over Westborough and Southborough to the east.

"Nell?" Violet walked softly down to the basement. "It's over. The sky is blue again."

Now, whenever a storm came up, Nell had to take refuge in the cellar, and no matter how kind and gentle her sister spoke to her or how many times she offered to stay beside her, Nell preferred to ride out the bad weather sitting alone in the rocking chair with the dog's head pressed onto her lap.

The blanket slipped off Nell's shoulders and she let out a long breath. "Will I ever stop reacting this way?"

Violet sat in the chair next to her sister. "It hasn't even been a year. You lived through a terrible, traumatic event. It's still raw. It will take time for the feelings to subside."

"I feel like a fool. I can't control my reaction." Nell ran her hands through her long auburn hair.

"It's not something you can control." Violet gave a half-smile. "If it was me, I'd pass out right onto the floor every time a storm came up and you'd have to revive me with smelling salts."

A little chuckle escaped from Nell's throat. "Maybe I should be more dramatic in my distress and not just sit rocking in a chair when a storm comes up."

The young women climbed the stairs to the shop and returned to their tasks.

Twenty-seven-year old Nell was an artist who sold original paintings in the store she shared with her sister. Violet, one year older, made handcrafted jewelry and pottery which she sold both online and in the shop.

After hanging a couple of new paintings on the walls, Nell returned to the back studio to work on a watercolor seascape. The early June sunlight streamed in through the windows calming her and banishing any remaining traces of nervousness that lingered after her storm-induced adrenaline rush.

Ever since she was able to hold a crayon or a brush, Nell loved to draw and sketch and paint and would spend hours each day hunched over her drawing pad creating colorful landscapes, portraits, and pictures of animals. *Colorful* really wasn't a strong enough word to describe Nell's pictures ... tree trunks weren't simply the chalky white of birch trees or the silvery gray of a Beech, or a mix of browns and tans and a little black of evergreens ... they were hues and tones of purples, pinks, and blues, or reds and greens and orange. In fact, every single object in a scene was awash in hundreds of shades of colors.

Nell's mother called her daughter's artwork impressionist in nature and when she asked Nell why she always drew things with so many colors, the little girl said, "Because that's what I see, Momma."

Sometimes, Nell got headaches and had to wear sunglasses in the house. Other times, when she went to the grocery store with her mother, she would become overwhelmed by the lights and the tall shelves and long tables filled with item after item.

Nell's mother became concerned and when she discussed her daughter's drawings and sensitivity to visual stimuli with the pediatrician, the doctor simply shrugged it off, but it all still picked at her until one day, Nell's art teacher took Mrs. Finley aside.

The teacher had suspicions about Nell and used a word Mrs. Finley had never heard before. *Tetrachromat.*

"A what?" Mrs. Finley asked, her eyes blinking in confusion.

"I really don't know anything about it," the teacher said, "but I've heard of people who have a fourth type of cone in their eyes. It's usually females who have it. The extra cones allow these people to see many, many more colors than ordinary people. They're called tetrachromats."

After hours of reading about having the extra type of cones in the eye, Mrs. Finley took Nell for testing and the researchers at the university confirmed the reason why the young girl drew and painted the way she did ... she was capable of seeing *millions* more colors than the average person could.

The little bell tinkled when the door of the shop opened and Nell could hear Violet speaking with a woman who had entered from Main Street.

For some reason, Nell wasn't able to focus on her painting and with a sigh, she lay down her brush and listened to Violet explain the stones and finishes of one of the necklaces to the customer.

Leaning forward to peek into the front room, Nell saw the woman from the back. She appeared to be in her mid-thirties, had shoulder-length black hair, was slender and well-dressed in tan slacks and a white blouse. The woman held the piece of jewelry to her neck and looked into a small mirror set on the jewelry case.

For a half-second, a blinding light sparked in Nell's vision. She blinked fast and rubbed at her eyelids, and when she glanced again at the woman standing in front of the jewelry counter, she nearly fell out of her seat.

The woman was awash in red ... her skin, her hair, her clothing ... everything was the same color ... bright, brilliant, blood red.

Nell had never experienced anything like it before. With her heart racing, she turned away and stared out the window for several seconds, then turned her head back to look in the front room.

The woman was still covered in red.

Nell's breathing rate increased and her heart pounded as she leapt from her chair and stepped back so she couldn't see the woman in the salesroom.

Her mind raced.

What's going on? Why am I seeing the woman this way? Why is she colored in red? Am I having a stroke?

Nell's stomach tightened. She could hear Violet ringing up a sale and placing something into a bag.

The woman thanked Violet for her help, said goodbye, and left the store.

Nell dashed out to the counter. "Did you see that woman?"

Violet looked up with a grin. "You mean the customer who was the only one in here? The one I was talking to? The woman I sold a necklace to? Yeah. I saw her." Violet's forehead wrinkled when she noticed the look on her sister's face. "What's wrong with you?"

"Nothing." Nell hurried to the door and took a quick look outside before turning around. "I...."

"What?" Violet came out from behind the counter.

"Was there anything unusual about that woman?"

"Unusual? Like what? She looked at the jewelry. She admired your artwork. She's going to come back. She wants to buy one of your smaller paintings."

"I only saw her from the back," Nell said. "Did she look funny from the front?"

Violet was growing concerned. "Funny how? What are you talking about?"

Nell cleared her throat and was about to explain what she'd seen when they heard the roar of a car engine.

Nell turned towards the sound. Through the window, she saw that a black sedan had pulled away from the curb and was hurtling away.

Someone yelled. A woman screamed. And then the terrible sound of a sickening thud filled the air.

Both sisters rushed to the door. Violet yanked it open.

Several people stood looking down at someone who lay in the middle of Main Street. It was the woman who had just been in the shop. She was on her back, her black hair spread out over the pavement, her right leg bent at an odd angle.

"Oh, no." Nell's words were like a whisper. She and Violet ran into the street to see if they could help.

A woman knelt beside the black-haired woman, blood pooling around her head.

"This woman stopped to help," someone told the sisters, gesturing to the kneeling woman. "She's a nurse. I called for an ambulance," another person informed them.

The nurse shook her head. "There's no pulse. There's a head injury. It's severe."

Violet grabbed Nell's arm. "How terrible."

Nell looked up and down the street. "Which car hit her?" she asked the people standing around.

A man said, "He took off. He sped away after he hit her."

Violet gasped and hustled her sister away from the crowd.

"Did you sense this was going to happen?" Violet asked, her eyes searching Nell's face.

Nell's eyes widened in surprise. "Of course not. I didn't sense a thing." A flush of fear ran through her veins.

Or did I?

2

Nell and Violet sat with mugs of tea at a long work table in the studio. Iris rested on the rug near the table staring up at the two women.

"Tell me again what happened when the woman was in here?" Violet had asked her sister when they returned to the shop after speaking with officers about the accident.

Nell went over the story for the third time explaining how the woman seemed to be covered in red. "I got panicky. I was afraid something was wrong with me. Everything else looked normal. It was just that woman who looked strange to me. She was red from head to toe."

Violet attempted to make sense of the odd

phenomenon. "Maybe the extra cones in your eyes went haywire."

"If the cones in my eyes went haywire, it would impact everything I see," Nell said. "My vision is the same no matter what I look at. It isn't one way for one thing and another way for everything else." Taking a sip of her tea, she placed the cup on the table and looked out the window at the garden in the backyard.

"When you looked at that woman, were you able to see her future?" Violet asked tentatively.

Nell moved her eyes to her sister's face. "See her future? I can only see more colors than regular people do. I'm not a psychic or a card reader or anything like that."

"Your vision changed after the tornado," Violet pointed out. "You could see even more colors than before. You got more sensitive to a lot of visuals. Your eyes get tired quicker. You need to rest them more. Maybe you've developed a new thing. Maybe now you can see other things ... like warnings."

Nell's eyes darkened. She wanted to dismiss her sister's crazy ideas and speculations, but she had to admit there could be a tiny grain of truth to what she was saying. "So you think the woman was giving off a warning and I saw it as red?" Nell shrugged. "But why would she give off a warning? How would she know she was about to be hit by a car? How could she know what was about to happen? And if she did know, wouldn't she have taken steps to prevent it?"

"Okay. You're right." Violet rubbed at her temple and pushed her long, straight, auburn hair from her face. "Maybe the woman didn't know anything at all. But, what if *possibilities* lurk on the air. What if things that *might* be about to happen float on the air all around us. You might be able to pick up on that. You might be able see things like that as colors."

"I don't like the sound of this." Nell's facial expression had changed from worried to frightened. "What am I supposed to do if I see someone covered in red again? Approach them and tell them they're in danger? I'll walk up to them and say, 'Hi. You're covered in red so something bad is about to happen to you.' You know how that would turn out. I'd end up in jail or the hospital or something. But how could I ignore it if I see something like that again? I'd know the person was in danger and I wouldn't be able to do anything about it?"

Violet let out a heavy sigh. "It seems like you'd have to warn them, but how could you do that? No one would believe you. They'd just think you were a nut."

"What am I going to do?" Nell rested her chin in her hand. "Maybe there's some way to avoid seeing warnings or danger coming from a person?"

Violet sat straighter. "Why don't you call Dr. Rob? He might know about things like this."

Thirty-five-year old, Dr. Rob Jennette had met Nell ten years ago when she was helping researchers at the university study tetrachromats. Jennette was an ophthalmologist and research scientist and, over the years, he and Nell had become close friends.

Nell raised an eyebrow. "I don't think Rob studies paranormal happenings. His work is rooted in science."

"If you told people thousands of years ago that one day men and women would fly in airplanes and have laptops and cell phones, they'd think all of that was paranormal," Violet said. "Paranormal stuff is only stuff we haven't figured out yet."

Nell grinned. "That's an interesting definition."

"Talk to Rob. He's up on all the latest cutting-edge research."

"I will. We're going to run together the day after tomorrow."

"Anyway...." Violet gave her sister a half-smile. "I hope you never see colors on me. And if you *do* see colors on me, you better make darned sure you tell me about it. Then I'll stay in the house for the rest of my life."

"What if the house is actually going to be the cause of your danger?" Nell asked.

Violet frowned. "Oh, I didn't think of that."

Nell smiled and then she picked up her mug with a hopeful expression. "I wonder if we're making more of this than it is. Maybe my eyes did get tired and for a few seconds, I saw red when I looked a certain distance away and that's why the woman was all one color. It might be an awful coincidence that she got hit by the car when she left the shop. We might be shaken up over nothing at all." Nell corrected herself. "I don't mean the woman's death was nothing at all. I mean my quirky vision might have been just a funky blip."

"Maybe that's what happened." Violet forced a smile, but Nell knew her sister was placating her, trying to make her feel less worried about what had happened.

"You're a good sister." Nell reached across the table and squeezed Violet's arm when an idea popped into her head. "What was the woman's name? Did she pay with a check or a credit card that had her name on it?"

"She paid with a credit card. Why do you want to know her name?"

"I'd like to know more about her," Nell said with a shrug.

The sisters went out to the front room and Violet took out the receipt of sale from the cash register. "Pepper Forrest."

Nell nodded. "Pepper is an unusual name."

"Maybe it was a nickname," Violet suggested. "But she used it on her credit card so maybe it was her real name."

"Let's look her up." Nell hurried into the studio room and sat in the desk chair in front of her laptop, and after a minute of looking at articles, she read aloud some information that had come up in the internet search. "Pepper Forrest was a professor of chemistry at Fuller University in Boston. She received a bachelor's degree from Stanford and a Ph.D. from MIT. She was originally from a small town in New Hampshire. She was the only child of a carpenter and a weaver. Dr. Forrest was thirty-four years old. She taught high school chemistry in California for several years before pursuing her doctorate."

Violet said, "Can you imagine someone hitting a

person crossing the street and then fleeing from the accident scene?"

"The driver must have panicked. Maybe he or she will come to their senses and turn themselves in," Nell said.

"After driving a few blocks, wouldn't you realize what you were doing and stop?"

"I hope I would. I guess you never know how you'll react until you're actually in the situation."

"You're being far too easy on this driver," Violet told her sister. "The repercussions will be far worse for the driver because he attempted to get away from what he did instead of staying at the scene and trying to help."

"I'm not being easy. The person *should* be punished for the hit and run," Nell said. "But I'm saying I understand how you could panic after an unexpected incident."

"I wonder if it was someone from town who hit the woman?" Violet asked. "Did you recognize the car as it sped down the street?"

"No." Nell shook her head. "It was all so fast. I barely noticed the color."

"It's more likely it was a tourist who did it," Violet speculated. "People who live in town know how crowded the streets can be. They know the rules and the speed limits. They'd be careful driving on Main Street. Even though it's only early June, there are still a lot of visitors in town. Residents all know these things."

Picking up the remote from the table, Nell said, "Let's put on the television. The local news station must be covering the story. Let's see what's being reported."

The television mounted on the far wall flicked on and the screen showed a news reporter standing in front of the Bluewater Police Station just beginning her report on the known details of the afternoon accident. "The victim's name is Pepper Forrest, a thirty-four-year-old chemistry professor at Fuller University in Boston."

A photo of Pepper Forrest displayed in the upper, right corner of the screen.

The reporter continued, "Dr. Forrest was visiting Bluewater and was shopping on Main Street when a speeding vehicle struck her as she crossed the road. Witnesses told authorities that the small, white sedan pulled away from its parking spot at high speed and sped towards the woman. There was no indication that the driver saw Dr. Forrest in the street and the car showed no signs of attempting to slow down."

"The driver must have been staring at his phone," Violet huffed.

Something about the on-air report picked at Nell.

"The vehicle fled the scene without stopping," the newscaster said.

"Maybe the witnesses were able to get the license plate number," Violet said as she looked to her sister for confirmation. "What do you think?"

Suddenly, Nell's green eyes widened. "The reporter said witnesses told the police the car was white."

"So?"

"The car I saw speeding past was black."

3

The sun was climbing into the bright blue sky promising an unusually hot day for so early in June when Violet and Nell walked into the busy coffee shop near the center of town. About twenty minutes north of Boston, Bluewater Cove, part of the city of Bluewater, was a popular tourist destination. With several pretty white sand beaches, the cozy, small village was full of restaurants, coffee and dessert shops, boutiques, a cliff walk along the sea, and a state park with hiking and biking paths winding for miles among the pines and deciduous trees.

The coffee shop was hopping with tourists and townsfolk who regularly congregated in the mornings to swap town news before heading off to work.

The sisters waved at some acquaintances and when they took two seats at a small recently vacated table, their friend, Dani, the owner, carried over mugs of coffee for them.

Tall, slim, and athletic, Dani was in her late twenties, had dark brown eyes and long, straight, blond hair that she wore up in a loose bun when she was working. She'd owned the coffee shop for five years and had built a reputation for serving delicious pastries and the best coffee for miles around.

"You must have heard the latest news," Dani said. "The place has been buzzing all morning about it."

"We know about the accident." Violet nodded and took a sip of the hot coffee.

"What's the latest?" Nell didn't want to tell Dani right away that Pepper Forrest had been in their store moments before getting hit by the car.

Dani said, "It was a hit and run. The victim died at the scene."

"Has the car been found? Has the driver been identified?" Nell asked. Waves of anxiety traveled through her body as they discussed the death of the tourist with Dani. Nell had tossed and turned all night trying to make sense of the experience of seeing the woman washed in red, but instead of better understanding what had happened, she only came up with more and more questions.

Dani lowered her voice and leaned in closer to her friends. "The police think the incident may have been deliberate."

Nell nearly tumbled off her seat. "Deliberate?" She was horrified that an unfortunate accident may have just become a murder.

"Why do they think that?" Violet questioned with wide eyes.

"There were no signs that the driver tried to brake before hitting the woman."

"But the person could have been texting on his or her phone," Nell suggested. "The driver may not have realized someone was in the road until he hit her."

Dani shook her head. "The police talked to a couple of witnesses. They claim the car pulled away from the curb just as Dr. Forrest stepped into the street. The driver floored it and drove right at the woman."

"Really?" Violet was so shocked by the turn of events that she didn't know what to say. "This is unbelievable. An intentional hit and run here in our little village of Bluewater Cove?"

"Gosh." Nell's stomach clenched and her head

spun with the new information. "Someone was watching and waiting for the woman?"

"So it seems." Dani moved away for several minutes to wait on some customers who wanted to order takeout beverages. When she returned, she said, "The police aren't releasing this information yet. They need to question more witnesses and a couple of accident specialists are coming to town to review the information to help make a determination. But really? They're leaning towards treating this as a murder."

Nell asked softly, "Did Peter tell you this?" Peter Bigelow was a Bluewater police officer and he and Dani had been dating for nearly ten years.

Dani made eye contact with her friend. "No comment."

"We'll take that as a *yes*," Violet said.

"You didn't hear it from me," Dani told them. "The department is trying to find out more about Dr. Forrest to determine if she had any enemies."

"Enemies?" Violet pondered the idea. "What could the woman have done to gain an enemy? She was a chemistry professor, not a lawyer or a probation officer or a doctor who made some mistakes."

"It could have been an old boyfriend or an ex-husband," Nell said. "Or someone she dated and broke off with. It could be a student in one of her classes who was unhappy about a grade."

"Angry over a grade?" Violet looked shocked. "Someone gets a bad grade and decides to kill the professor? What's the world coming to?"

"The world is full of nuts," Dani said. "There's no shortage of crazy people."

Nell said to their friend, "The woman was in our shop. Violet helped her pick out a necklace."

"The victim? Dr. Forrest?" Dani's eyebrows raised at the news. "She was in your store yesterday?"

With a nod, Nell said, "She was in the shop right before she crossed the street."

A little gasp escaped from Dani's throat. "She left your store, crossed the street, and got killed?"

Violet gave a sad nod. "She bought a necklace. She told me she was going to come back to buy one of Nell's paintings."

The sisters had thought the death was a terrible incident of misfortune, even talking about how the woman would still be alive if she'd stayed in the shop just a little longer. Now they realized that timing had nothing to do with it. Someone had been waiting for Dr. Forrest. Someone had planned to kill her. Someone had waited outside like a venomous spider for their victim to pass in front of them. The thought chilled Nell and Violet to the bone.

"Do the police know she was in the shop right before she was struck by that car?" Dani asked.

Nell almost winced from hearing the word, *killed*. "We gave statements when the police arrived. We were outside in the street. We ran out to see if we could help, but it was too late. Dr. Forrest was already dead. We told Officer Michaels that the woman had been shopping in our store right before she crossed the street."

"Wow," Dani muttered. "Peter didn't tell me that. How did Dr. Forrest seem when she was with you? Did she seem nervous?"

"I was working in the studio in the backroom," Nell said. "Violet waited on her."

"I didn't notice any odd behavior. The woman didn't seem nervous to me. Although...." Violet let her voice trail off.

"Although what?" Nell asked turning to her sister.

"I remember she kept glancing out of the window. I thought she was looking out at the shops on the street around ours. It was a really nice day. I thought she was admiring the town on a sunny day. I didn't think she seemed nervous though, but ... maybe she was."

"I wonder if she was suspicious of something," Nell said, her mind racing over the details of the incident. "Maybe she thought she recognized someone or maybe, she noticed a car that drove by. Maybe she was alerted by something she saw and got a little worried so she kept looking out the windows."

"That could be," Dani agreed. "You should tell Peter how she was acting."

"It might have been nothing though," Violet said.

"There's probably nothing about this situation that is meaningless," Dani said. "Let the police decide what's important and what isn't. You know Peter says that one little thing we all ignore can be the key to blowing a case wide open."

"I'll talk to him," Violet promised.

With a nod, Dani started away from the table. "I need to get back to work or Lucy and Liz will quit on me. We'll talk later."

Violet's face looked pale when she turned her attention to Nell. "I can't believe this. Someone hit that woman on purpose. The whole thing was planned. The driver intended to kill Dr. Forrest."

Nell's lower lip trembled slightly. "I wish I could

have warned her. The red color that washed over her must have been from the anxiety she was feeling about someone she noticed outside. She must have been giving off worry or nervousness and I picked up on it by seeing color all around her."

"It must have been very strong for you to be able to see it," Violet said staring down at her coffee mug trying to make sense of what was going on.

"If I had warned her...." Nell said with a shaky voice.

Violet lifted her eyes. "There's no way you could have given her a warning. Do you really think she would have heeded it? She would have run away from you and your nutty suggestion."

Nell sighed and rubbed at her forehead. "I've always kind of felt like an outsider because of my ability to see so many more colors than the average person. I love all the colors and I'm grateful to be able to see the exceptional beauty in the world, but it does sometimes make me feel separated from everyone else. If this new thing I've developed can help people avoid danger or tragedy or loss, I have to find a way to give them that message. I need to figure out a way to tell them so they'll believe me. Then I can help keep people safe and nothing like this will happen again."

Thinking of Nell's headaches and how hard it sometimes was for her to be in places with lots of visual stimuli like markets, restaurants, amusement parks, schools, sports stadiums, or museums, Violet gave her sister a loving look. "I'm sorry that seeing colors can be hard on you. You're the best person I know. You always want to help. You always want things to be better for people. Talk to Dr. Rob. We'll figure out this new thing you have ... and we'll do it together."

4

Thirty-five-year-old, Dr. Rob Jennette taught at an optometry school located in Bluewater and conducted research there and at a prominent Cambridge university and hospital. Nell and Dr. Rob had become friends when, ten years ago, he assisted with her month's-long evaluation into the qualities of her vision. The two met up a few times each week to go running together.

When Nell arrived at Rob's office, he was sitting at his desk wearing a t-shirt and running shorts typing furiously at his laptop. He was so engrossed in his work that he didn't hear Nell come in, and when she spoke, he nearly flew out of his chair.

"You scared me." Rob shook his head and took in a deep breath. "Sorry. I lost track of the time." The doctor, just under six feet tall, had dark brown hair, warm brown eyes, and was slim and fit.

"At least you didn't forget about our run." Nell smiled and sat down in the chair next to the desk. Rob could be forgetful at times and more than once, he wasn't in the office when Nell came to meet him.

"That only happened once," Rob said in his own defense.

"Hmm. Way more than once, but I know who I'm dealing with so I let it go."

A tall man with a medium-build, short brown hair and blue eyes stood at the door to Rob's office and seemed taken aback by Nell and Rob dressed in running clothes.

"Am I interrupting?" The man's face was serious.

"Not at all. We're just about to go out for some exercise," Rob said. "Atkins, this is Ellen Finley. Nell, this is our new ophthalmologist, Dr. Atkins Murray."

Nell stood to shake hands. "Nice to meet you. Call me Nell."

The new doctor shook with her and then quickly turned back to Rob. "I wanted to discuss a few things with you. Another time." He whirled on his heel and left the room without saying another word leaving Nell staring after him with a look of surprise.

"Don't mind him. Let's go for our run." Rob took

his keys from the desk and he and Nell left the five-story brick building and began to jog through the campus past tall trees, lush, manicured lawns, and beds blooming with late spring flowers. They crossed the street and headed into the north end of the state park to run along the trails.

"What's up with that new doctor?" Nell asked between breaths.

"Atkins is brilliant, a highly regarded researcher and teacher," Rob said. "He can be awkward and abrupt."

"He certainly can," Nell chuckled.

"He also has a very high opinion of himself."

"From our two-second interaction, I'm not surprised." As they ran through the woods, Nell admired the pastel colors running over the trunks of the trees and the silver, gold, and pinks in the sunlight filtering down through the leaves.

After the first mile, Nell's muscles warmed, her breathing evened out, and her movement fell into a natural, comfortable rhythm.

"What an awful thing about that professor who got killed in the hit and run accident," Rob said. "The reports made it sound like it happened right outside of your shop. Where you there when it happened?"

Nell said, "I want to talk to you about that."

"You do?" Rob sounded surprised. "What about it?"

Nell told him what had happened when the woman came into the store. "I was working in the studio backroom and Violet was out front in the store. I heard the little bell over the door chime when someone came in. I glanced up from the painting I was working on just as the woman approached one of the jewelry counters to browse." Nell paused for a few moments before continuing. "I'd never seen anything like what I saw that day."

Rob looked at Nell out of the corner of his eye.

"The woman was washed all over in red, from the tip of her head all the way down to her shoes. Her hair, her skin, her clothing, everything. It was as if someone held a red film over her, or like a television malfunctioned and the character on the screen was tinted completely red," Nell said.

Rob slowed his pace to a walk and stopped. Nell followed his lead. "Has this ever happened before? Even a little bit?" The doctor stared into his friend's face.

"Never," Nell said flatly as she rubbed at her eyes. "I would have told you if it had."

"This is remarkable. How did you feel when this was happening?" Rob asked.

"I felt frightened, shocked, dismayed, confused," Nell said softly as her mind relived the experience of seeing the red-tinted woman in the shop. "For a few seconds, I thought I was losing my mind ... or having a stroke or something. I didn't understand what was happening. I still don't. Was it a warning of danger? It must have been because something awful happened to her. Could I have intervened? Could I have told her she was in danger?"

"I don't know how you could have done that," Rob said gently. "If a stranger came up to you right now and told you that he could sense danger all around you, would you accept that? Would you think he was crazy? You wouldn't believe him, would you?"

"I think I would now," Nell admitted, "after seeing that woman covered in red. Maybe I would take the man's warning to heart."

"Well, I wouldn't believe anyone who told me something like that. It's too farfetched to believe. My point being that you couldn't have helped that woman. Dr. Forrest wouldn't have accepted what you told her. So wipe the guilt off the slate. It isn't helpful."

"That's kind of harsh," Nell said with a frown.

"I don't mean it to be. I know the experience is upsetting. You could not prevent the car from hitting the woman. You need to focus on what you *can* understand. Let's analyze the facts and details. Let's consider what might be done should this happen again. We'll go at this rationally. Let's work to figure this out."

"Sometimes, your scientific way of thinking can come off as cold," Nell said.

"Science is a way to understand the world," Rob said calmly. "It's a tool to make sense and order out of chaos. Talk to me about what was going on with you right before this happened."

Nell sighed. "I was at the shop with Violet. That was the morning of the big thunderstorm."

"Ah, I see." Rob knew about Nell's lingering anxiety over storms of any kind. "Were your feelings of fear during the storm stronger than usual?"

"No, about the same."

"Did you go down to the basement?"

"Yes. The same as always," Nell said.

"Did you remember anything new about the tornado?" Rob asked.

"Nothing. As soon as the storm passed, I went upstairs and went to work in the studio."

"Was Iris with you in the basement?"

"Yes, but Violet doesn't come down with me anymore. I told her I could handle it without her."

"That's progress then."

Nell had to think about that. "Yeah, I guess it is."

"So you were alone with the dog in a scary situation," Rob pointed out, "but you rode it out. What about your vision? Was anything different?"

"No. I closed my eyes. I could still see colors with my eyes shut, just like always, but they were muted like they always are when my eyes are closed. My vision was the same as it always is. Nothing was different."

"How about at the studio? Did you notice anything different about what you were seeing when you were working?"

"Nothing stood out to me. I didn't notice anything different. My eyes were tired though," Nell told the scientist. Sometimes, the young woman needed a break from all the color she could see in the world and so she retreated to a white or cream-colored room, or when that wasn't possible, she would close her eyes from the overwhelming sensory input and rest.

Rob's forehead knitted together in thought and he breathed deeply. "The woman who was killed may have been in some kind of distress. Maybe she was giving off some energy ... some energy like the radiation wavelengths of the visible spectrum, and you were able to pick up on that energy and see it as red."

Nell stared at the man. "Huh."

"You're very articulate," Rob deadpanned.

Nell shook her head. "I understand what you said, but is that possible? Did I notice the woman's distress and actually see it coming off of her as color?"

"It's an intriguing possibility," Rob said. "It would be interesting to test. Would you be willing to undergo an evaluation to determine if you're able to see emotions given off as visible energy?"

Nell's face hardened. "You know I don't like being treated like a lab rat." When Nell was in her late teens, she agreed to testing with several doctors and researchers, and Rob was among them. The experience confirmed the earlier testing done when she was a child. She was a tetrachromat, but the extended research made her feel like a *thing* and not a human being ... like a freak in a circus sideshow act. "You think about what I'd need to do in a testing situation and then I'll consider it."

Rob said, "As you know, most people have three

kinds of cones in their eyes. You have four." Cones were structures that are adjusted to absorb certain wavelengths of light. "The extra cone in your eyes could be giving you the capability to perceive more dimensions of energy. Dr. Forrest's distress may have created energy that was visible to a tetrachromat. It's certainly a compelling theory."

"Compelling to you." Nell shook her head. "Strange and terrible to me."

5

Looking over the menus, Nell and Violet sat at a table on the outside deck of a popular restaurant right at the water's edge. The sun was slowly setting and lavender, pink, and dark blue brush strokes decorated the sky.

"What a beautiful evening," Violet said admiring the view. "Tell me what you see," she said to her sister. Violet enjoyed listening to Nell describe all the colors she saw in the world and tried to imagine what it would be like to be able see millions more shades and hues painting the landscape.

Nell smiled and attempted to describe what she could see. "What you perceive as lavender, I see as lots of different streaks of colors together ... pinks, reds, purples, some red, even some gold."

Violet rested her chin in her hand as she gazed out over the ocean and sighed. "Your description sounds like some gorgeous, amazing, wonderland. I love to hear about what you're seeing." Over the years, Nell and Violet had described to each other the colors they could see. Nell learned what was visible to her sister and used Violet's words for colors to explain what she herself was experiencing so Violet might have a better understanding of Nell's perception.

"I wish I could see the way you do," Violet said.

Nell gave her sister a look.

"Oh, I know. It can be overwhelming. But for just one day, I wish I could be you."

The waiter came by and took drink orders and when he left their table, Violet asked, "Did you see the latest news report?"

Nell didn't have to ask what the topic of the article might be. For the past few days, all the news they were interested in had to do with Dr. Pepper Forrest.

"What does it say?" Nell braced herself for the information.

"It has a picture of Dr. Forrest and the police ask if anyone recognizes her or if anyone knows where she was staying while here in town, to get in touch with them," Violet said while passing her phone to her sister. "Here's a good picture of her."

For a second, Nell hesitated and wouldn't accept the phone. She didn't want to see the face of the woman who had died right outside of their shop. Besides the small, grainy photograph shown on television, Nell remembered she'd only seen Dr. Forrest's face in death.

"Have a look," Violet encouraged.

Nell reluctantly took the phone and when she saw the picture of Pepper Forrest, a wave of sadness rushed through her.

An attractive woman smiled from the phone screen. With ebony hair, fair skin, and bright eyes brimming with warmth and intelligence, Dr. Forrest projected a friendly, outgoing, caring nature.

Violet searched her sister's face. "Is she covered in red in the picture?"

Nell shook her head and handed the phone back. "She looks normal. No red at all. The picture is just black and white." After a pause, Nell said, "She looks like a nice person."

"I thought the same thing," Violet agreed. "So the question is, why would someone want to kill a nice person?"

A woman's voice asked, "Who's a nice person?" Dani stood at their table smiling at the sisters.

"We didn't notice you," Nell said.

Dani took a seat. "Not surprised. You both look knee-deep in a serious conversation."

"We were talking about the murder case," Violet informed the young woman. "Does Peter know anything more?"

Dani took a sip from Nell's water glass. "Peter's running late. He's meeting me here. Can I sit with you until he arrives? You can ask him if he has any new information about the professor."

"Of course you can sit with us," Nell said. "Have you heard anything from Peter about the case? Are the police close to making an arrest?"

Dani rolled her eyes. "No way. They still haven't found the car that hit Dr. Forrest. The case sounds like a mess. Peter's been stressed out over it."

Violet handed their friend her phone with the picture of Pepper Forrest on the screen. "We think she looks like a nice person. We were talking about who would want to kill her."

Dani took a look. "She was pretty. She looks full of life in that photo."

"Do the police still think the incident was intentional?" Nell questioned.

"They do, yes."

"Have they found anything in her background that suggests someone might want her dead?"

"I haven't heard anything about that." Dani ordered a drink from the waiter when he came to the table to take the sisters' dinner orders. "Peter's careful about sensitive information. I sometimes can put two and two together by what he says and by what he leaves out. I hear him on the phone with the other officers and I can figure out some things from the one-sided conversation."

Nell looked at Dani with a serious expression. "Something unusual happened when Dr. Forrest was in the store right before she was hit."

Narrowing her eyes, Dani said, "I don't like the sound of this. What happened?"

Nell and Violet took turns reporting the details of Dr. Forrest's visit to the shop, what Nell saw, and what happened when the professor left the store.

Although Dani was aware that Nell was a tetrachromat, she knew this experience was out of the ordinary for her friend ... *way* out of the ordinary. "What the heck? How could you see that?"

Nell told Dani about Dr. Rob's theory that Pepper Forrest was upset or frightened and gave off her emotions in waves of energy that Nell could see.

Dani didn't say anything for a few moments. "Is that possible? Someone can actually *see* another person's emotional state?"

"It's a theory," Nell said. "Rob is going to do some research on it. He might want to do some experiments with me. I'm not sure if I'm willing to do that."

"It would be pretty incredible if you could see how people were feeling. It makes some sense though, doesn't it?" Dani asked. "There are different kinds of energy. You see more colors than we do. Why wouldn't it be possible for some people to interpret the energy we might be giving off?"

Violet leaned forward. "But why couldn't Nell see energy like that before this woman came into the store?"

"Maybe the woman had more powerful energy flowing from her," Dani guessed. "If the professor was concerned for her safety, her emotions must have been in high gear. I bet Nell never met a person who thought someone might be out to kill her."

Nell's eyes widened. "Good point. I never have."

Violet said, "I have an idea. I suspect Nell became more sensitive to things after living through that tornado. She feared for her life. Traumatic events can change a person."

"My new skill might be a result of both things,"

Nell said. "I've become more sensitive from being in the tornado and Dr. Forrest was giving off a tremendous amount of nervous energy that I was able to see."

Violet began to nod her head in agreement, but then stopped. "Wait a minute."

Dani and Nell turned their eyes to the young woman.

Looking directly at her sister, Violet said, "You told me you thought the car that hit Dr. Forrest was black in color."

Nell's face began to pale.

"But the witnesses report the car was white," Violet added. "You saw a different color than what was really there. Why would that happen?"

"I have no idea," Nell muttered.

"It's simple," Dani said. "Whoever was driving that car must have been full of fury and had only one intention ... to take the professor's life. The energy the driver was giving off was dark and full of hatred so the car appeared black to Nell."

"That actually makes sense," Nell said with a look of surprise. "Maybe you and Rob should work together to figure this thing out."

Dani smiled. "Rob's lab couldn't afford to pay me what I'm worth."

Violet asked, "Did you tell Rob you saw the car in a color different from what it really was?"

"It slipped my mind," Nell said. "He was talking about light energy and the visible part of the light spectrum and coming up with ideas and theories about how I managed to see what I saw. Then he came up with the suggestion that we do some testing and I sort of shut down. You know how I dislike being the subject of experiments. I completely forgot about seeing the car as black."

The Bluewater police chief came out to the deck following the hostess to a table in the corner and every person sitting outside eyed him and began to whisper with their dinner partners. The chief was with a slim, fit man about six feet tall with light brown hair and brown eyes.

Dani leaned forward. "That's the detective from Boston who came up to help out on the case. Peter says the guy has a lot of experience and will be a great asset to the team."

"He's not bad looking either." Violet winked at her friend and her sister. "What's his name?"

"Michael Gregory," Dani told them. "I think he plans to speak with everyone who was at the accident scene so he'll probably be paying you both a visit sometime soon."

"Too bad I'm seeing someone," Violet joked. "He's pretty cute."

"Well, Nell isn't seeing anyone at the moment." Dani made eye contact with Nell and gave her a playful little nudge with her elbow.

Nell shook her head. "I've got plenty on my mind right now. I'm not looking for a romantic involvement."

"Well, things can change quickly," Dani said with a grin.

"That's for sure." Nell groaned thinking about her unwelcome new *ability* and how it showed up out-of-the-blue. Taking a quick glance over to the table where the police chief and the detective were sitting, Detective Gregory caught Nell's eye and held her gaze for a couple of seconds longer than he should have.

Feeling a warm flush dart over her skin, Nell broke eye contact with the man and looked away, giving herself a mental shake.

Oh, no. Not now.

6

———

S tanding at the door of the shop, Iris wagged her tail and gave a welcoming yip causing Nell and Violet, who were hanging some new artwork to display for sale, to look over at the dog.

"Who's coming?" Nell asked the dog cheerfully and as soon as she spoke the question, Dani opened the door and walked in.

Iris wiggled and wagged at the blond woman and Dani knelt down to scratch the dog's head cooing over the friendly animal. "A greeting like this never gets old," she smiled.

"What brings you by so early?" Violet asked their friend. "Aren't you supposed to be at the coffee shop?"

"I'm on my way, but I wanted to share some information with you."

Nell's heart started to race.

Dani said, "The police have located the car that hit Pepper Forrest. It was in a parking lot at the back of the Burlington Mall. The car was a rental, and the police believe the man who rented it used a false driver's license and a false credit card. The name on the license was Justin Carr."

"Have the police located the man?" Nell asked hopefully.

"He hasn't been found. Police ran the information they obtained from the car rental company and the man who leased the car does not seem to have any history. The police have a theory that the man in the driver's license photo may have been wearing a disguise and he was probably in disguise when he hit Dr. Forrest. If that idea is true, then the driver certainly intended to kill her."

"This gets weirder and weirder." Violet shook her head.

Nell asked, "Have the police learned anything about the professor that would explain someone's desire to kill her?"

"No, and there's a lot of pressure on law enforcement to solve this mess," Dani told them. "Peter is straight out. He's working double shifts. Tourist season is gearing up and the mayor wants the killer found so the town doesn't suffer an economic downturn when people decide to go elsewhere for vacation."

"Are there any leads at all?" Nell questioned.

"None." Dani checked the time. "I need to get to work, but I wanted to tell you something else. Pepper Forrest was staying at the edge of town at that really swanky bed and breakfast, the Sandy Rose." The Rose, well-known all around the country, was a very expensive inn with beautiful period furnishings set on an acre of land and surrounded by extensive lawns and gorgeous gardens. "I know your parents were friendly with the innkeeper. Why don't you call him and see if you can stop by to talk to him about Dr. Forrest before all the news people descend on the man?"

"You're amazing." Nell thanked their friend for her help.

Violet hurriedly called the innkeeper, William Mathers, and when she ended the call, she told Nell, "He's waiting for us. He said we'd better hurry over." Violet hung the *Closed* sign in the window and the sisters headed out.

The Sandy Rose Inn had a huge wrap-around

porch and tall Beech trees stood on each side of the place providing welcoming shade on hot days. Flowers bloomed in pots set on the steps and on the porch, and spring flowers spilled over the sides of the boxes at the windows. White rockers stood on the porch waiting for guests to come and sit for a while. At the northern edge of Bluewater Cove, the inn was located on a quiet road that led down to a sandy beach.

William Mathers, in his early seventies, tall and slender with white hair and pale blue eyes, had owned the bed and breakfast for over forty years. When he purchased it, the old house had fallen into disrepair, but within two years, he'd returned it to its former glory and had even won an award for the historical preservation.

William greeted the sisters as they walked up the porch steps. "Every time I see you two, you look more and more like your beautiful mother." William and his wife had been friends for decades with Nell and Violet's parents and he'd known the girls since they were little.

After exchanging hugs, he said, "Let's go inside. The police chief warned me the news outlets would arrive like a tsunami once they got wind that Dr. Forrest had been a guest here."

Taking seats on comfortable sofas in the lovely sunroom at the back of the house, they discussed Pepper Forrest.

"When Dr. Forrest first arrived, we chatted a little, but she didn't seem eager to talk. She was certainly polite and well-mannered, but she kept to herself. In the mornings, she rose early and ate a quick breakfast in the morning room. She didn't linger over coffee or to speak with the other guests ... she just went in and out. She either returned to her room for a while or went out for the day."

"How long was she here at the B and B?" Nell asked.

"Two nights before the accident happened. She was planning to stay one more night."

"Did she arrive by car?" Violet asked.

"She didn't have a vehicle," William said. "She arrived by taxi. I believe she used the town shuttle when she left the inn or called a car service to take her where she wanted to go."

"Did anyone come to collect her things from the room?" Nell questioned. "Did a friend or relative come here?"

"Not yet." William shook his head sadly. "The police confiscated some of the items from the room. I suppose they took some of the things to look for information about any family or friends they might contact. Such a terrible tragedy. The woman goes on a short break and ends up dead."

"Did you talk to Dr. Forrest about why she was here? Why did she choose Bluewater Cove?" Nell asked.

"Dr. Forrest told me she lived and worked in Boston," William said. "She told me she hadn't been on a vacation for years. She was always working. Dr. Forrest decided to come to town because she wanted to attend a symposium at the medical school here and take an extra day to relax."

"Did she mention any family? A husband? Children? Siblings?" Violet asked. "Did she talk about any friends?"

William shook his head. "She didn't say a word to me about any relatives or friends. She came here alone. Perhaps, she met someone here in town or at the symposium, but I don't know anything about that."

"So the main reason for her visit was to attend the conference?" Nell asked.

"That was my impression," William told the sisters. "But as I said, our interactions were limited and formal in nature."

"How did the professor seem when you spoke with her?" Nell asked. "Did she seem worried or nervous? Did you notice her acting concerned about her surroundings? Maybe careful of who was close by?"

"Really, I didn't. She didn't want to linger in the breakfast room or in the common areas. I never noticed her outside by the gardens. Most visitors enjoy relaxing in the chairs by the flowers or under the trees or by the pond," William said. "At the very least, the guests enjoy the front porch. I never saw Dr. Forrest relaxing outside. That made me think she wanted to visit as many places in town as she could. Perhaps, she wasn't one for the beach or didn't care to spend time in nature. Some people prefer museums and historical landmarks or restaurants and shops."

"Did Dr. Forrest ask you for any tips on area sightseeing?" Violet questioned.

"She didn't. She seemed to have a plan of what she wanted to do. I did ask if I could point out places of interest, but she told me she was all set."

"Did she ask you for directions to any place in particular?" Nell asked.

"She didn't. She did ask about the trolley system and I gave her a pamphlet with information on the routes and the cost," William said, "but that was really all she asked me about."

"Did any of the guests talk to Dr. Forrest more than the others did?" Violet questioned. "Did she seem more comfortable with any of the guests?"

William started to shake his head, but stopped. "One of the guests was a lovely older woman. She was the only one who seemed to connect with Dr. Forrest. They didn't speak at length as far as I know, but they did seem to enjoy speaking to each other."

Nell asked with excitement in her voice, "Is that guest still here?"

"I'm afraid not. She left on the morning of the accident. She lives in New York City."

Nell's heart sank with disappointment, and then she asked a question that had been picking at her. "Did you happen to notice anyone lurking around the inn? Did you notice the same car driving by multiple times or maybe, someone walking by giving the inn more interest than is usual for a tourist?"

William's bushy white eyebrows went up. "No, I didn't. Do you think the driver of the car that hit Dr. Forrest might have been looking for her here? Do you think she was in some kind of danger?"

"We're only speculating and grasping at straws," Violet told the man.

"May I ask why you're interested in the woman?"

Nell swallowed hard. "She was in our shop minutes before being hit by the car. She died in the road right outside the shop. We went out to offer help, but she was already dead."

"How terrible. I'm so sorry you had to see that," William said kindly. "Is there a concern that the hit and run wasn't an accident?"

"It's a possibility," Violet said carefully.

The three talked for a few more minutes, and then as Nell and Violet were about to leave, William said, "Funny thing. I could be wrong about it, but I'm not sure."

"Wrong about what?" Nell asked, a shiver of unease rolling over her skin.

"When I was upstairs the other day making up one of the guest rooms, I thought I could hear Dr. Forrest in her room. I thought I could hear her crying."

7
___

Nell sat at a café table on the patio of a sandwich shop in the center of town eating a mozzarella and tomato sandwich and reading on her laptop. She'd worked a long day at the studio and decided to take Iris for a walk along the beach before heading into town for a bite to eat.

Iris enjoyed resting at Nell's feet on the patio watching all the people strolling to the shops and restaurants and down to the harbor to see the boats. The dog was always friendly and well-behaved in public and was welcome in many of the town's establishments. Nell and Violet often joked that people were happier to see Iris than they were to see them.

Even though Nell had read many articles and

papers on tetrachromats, she still looked at fresh research for new information on the uncommon ability. Losing track of time, she'd sat for two hours on the patio scouring the internet for new material about tetrachromatism and for articles on what ancient peoples believed colors represented.

Letting out a sigh, Nell looked down at Iris who had glanced up when she heard the long breath of air. "Reading about colors just makes me more confused."

Nell realized she and the dog were the only ones left outside and that darkness had fallen while she'd been doing her research. "We better get back," she told the dog, gathering up her things.

Walking along the brick sidewalks heading back to the house, Nell and Iris passed through the cozy town under the old-fashioned streetlamps. A chill made Nell shiver a little and she wished she'd thought to bring her sweater. The town was quieter than it would be in a few weeks when schools let out and families and couples started their summer vacations in earnest. Nell loved the month of June ... the weather was warm, the days were longer, the town was beginning to buzz with activity, she and Violet could enjoy a swim in the cold ocean water, she could bike and run on the park's paths, and the summer months stretched far out in front of her.

Nell and Iris turned down a side road that would lead to the house's rear door. The home had been passed down from her grandmother to her mother and now to her and Violet. The family's main residence had been in central Massachusetts, but the Bluewater Cove house was where they spent most summers and many weekends.

The house had been added-on to so that part of it faced Main Street and the back section faced a quiet neighborhood lane. The Main Street part housed the studio and the shop, and the rest of the house was used as their residence. There was a big yard enclosed by a fence so Iris could go out whenever she wanted to without one of the sisters needing to accompany her.

Walking along, Nell chattered to the dog, thinking out loud. "Colors are related to different things. Take red for instance, in some cultures it stands for anger and rage, and in another society it stands for courage, life, and victory. It can also mean death or can be used to symbolize protected health. If colors mean so many different things, how will I know what they mean when I see them?"

Iris gave Nell a sympathetic look.

"You know what black can mean? This one is confusing, too. Black can refer to evil and death and mystery, but to other people it can mean resurrection and life. Completely different things. The same color. How can I figure this out?" Nell shook her head. "For the rest of the night, I'm taking a break from thinking about this stuff."

Iris let out a soft yip.

"I'm glad you agree," Nell said. "I wonder when Violet will get back?"

Violet had gone out on a date to a movie and dinner with someone she'd met a month ago.

"I can't wait to get into my pajamas and collapse on the sofa." Nell stopped short. Her house was two homes away from where she stood.

For a moment, Nell was sure she saw a flash of orange in the windows. *Could it have been a flicker of fire?* She watched closely, waiting to see if something flashed again.

Nothing. The house looked fine.

Nell took an anxious glance at the dark sky afraid what she saw had been a bolt of lightning, but the stars shone down and the inky sky was clear.

Iris whined and some fur on her back stood up.

Just as Nell was about to start walking again, she spotted what looked like a shadow darting into the bushes that separated her house from the neighbor's home.

Iris growled low and deep causing goosebumps to form over Nell's arms.

"What is it, girl?" Nell whispered. "Is someone in our yard?"

On the neighbor's front porch, a man called out. "Who's there?"

"It's me, Mr. Patrick. It's Nell. And Iris." She hurried past her house to talk to the neighbor, a short, spry, seventy-eight-year-old man named John Patrick. John had lived in his home for over forty years with his wife, Ida.

John said, "I thought I saw someone in your side yard. I guess it was only you."

A shiver moved over Nell's arms. "It wasn't me. We're just getting home from the center of town. We were walking back from the sandwich shop."

Nell could see Mr. Patrick standing under the porch light and she watched as his eyes narrowed. "I'm pretty sure I saw someone in your side yard. I thought it looked like a man."

A surge of anger pulsed through Nell's veins. "Where did he go?" she asked. "Did you see which way he went?"

Mr. Patrick huffed. "When I came out to the

porch, I didn't see him anywhere. Maybe it was a stray shadow or a cloud passing over the moon."

Taller and sturdier than her husband, seventy-six-year-old Ida Patrick came out from their living room carrying a heavy hammer. "Let's go make sure no one is in Nell's house."

Iris sniffed at the ground and trotted into the bushes before crossing the Patricks' front lawn and sniffing hurriedly along the road. The dog followed the lane past two houses and then she stopped, threw back her head, and let out a wolf-like howl.

The sound made Nell's heart race. "Iris seems to think whoever or whatever was here has left."

Clutching the hammer, Ida Patrick said, "So it seems, but we'll go with you to check the house anyway. Just to be sure."

"Okay." Feeling edgy, and despite having the dog with her, Nell was happy to have the Patricks come into the house to be sure it was all clear. Before going inside, she took a look back to the road and a quick orange flash shot up from the ground like a rocket and, in a millisecond, it disappeared into the night air.

Nell gasped.

Mrs. Patrick heard the young woman's distress and thought it was caused by the idea that someone might be lurking inside. "Don't worry, hon. We won't leave you until we're sure the house is safe. No one is going to mess with three people and a dog."

After checking each room, Nell offered the Patricks some tea, but they declined and returned to their own home, but not before insisting that Nell call them should she feel uneasy or worried about anything at all.

"We can be here in three seconds," Mrs. Patrick told her. "People think we're old and slow. Well, we may be old, but we're quick and spry and not afraid to give some creep what-for." The older woman raised her hammer to make the point.

When Violet returned from her date and heard someone may have been lurking around in the yard, she rushed from room to room pulling down the shades. "Who could it have been? Why would anyone be skulking around our yard?"

"It was probably nothing at all." Nell wanted to convince her sister as well as herself, but couldn't quite wipe the worry from her mind since both she and Mr. Patrick thought they'd seen someone moving around outside the house. "Or some kids felt like getting into some mischief."

"I don't like it." Violet stood in the living room

with her arms wrapped around her body. "At least, we have Iris. She won't let anything happen to us."

Iris thumped her tail against the wood floor.

"It couldn't have anything to do with Pepper Forrest, could it?" Violet asked.

Nell's heart dropped down to her fuzzy, slipper-covered feet. The same thought had crossed her mind. "I don't see how it could. We don't know anything. We weren't even outside when the accident happened. No one would connect us to Dr. Forrest. Why would they?"

"Because you saw her covered in red," Violet said.

"No one knows that," Nell protested.

"Dr. Rob knows it. Dani knows it. Maybe Rob told that snooty, strange new doctor about it. Then that guy told other people, and on and on. Maybe Dani told Peter and Peter told the other officers."

"Peter wouldn't tell anyone," Nell said.

"Someone could have overheard us talking about it," Violet said.

"If someone overheard that conversation, they wouldn't have understood it. They wouldn't have any idea what we were talking about."

When Violet sank into one of the soft chairs and

sighed, Nell decided it was time to tell her sister more about the night.

"When Iris and I were outside, I saw an orange flickering light inside our windows."

Violet didn't say anything, but she looked like she might be feeling a little bit ill.

"Then I saw a flash of orange light shoot up from the ground right before I came inside," Nell said.

Violet stared. "Is there anything else? Did you see anything else that was strange?"

"That's all."

"I guess that was enough for one evening." Violet shook her head. "Actually, that was enough for a lifetime. What's going on?"

Nell explained that earlier, she'd done some research on colors and their meanings.

"What does the color orange mean?" Violet asked.

"Orange means a warning," Nell said.

"Great. Does it have any other meanings?"

"I only found the one thing, a warning."

Violet looked at Iris sitting on her dog bed in the corner and then made eye contact with her sister. "Two dogs would be more protection. Maybe we should get another dog."

8

The next afternoon, William Mathers, the owner of The Sandy Rose, phoned Nell to ask if she might come to the inn. A friend of Pepper Forrest was there asking about the woman and Mr. Mathers thought it would be helpful if Nell or Violet could speak with her.

Violet stayed behind to mind the shop, and when Nell arrived at the inn, she ran into the gardener and handyman, Bobby, who was working near the white picket fence tending the roses.

"Afternoon." Bobby touched the brim of his wide straw hat.

"The gardens look beautiful." Nell admired the flowers running along the fence. "You certainly have a magic touch. Our gardens are pretty, but nothing at all like these."

"It takes a lot of time," Bobby told her. The thirty-five-year-old gardener had worked at the inn for several months and his skin was perpetually tanned from his outdoor work. He was medium-height, had thin with wiry muscles, brown hair and brown eyes. "If you want me to come by your house and offer some suggestions, I'd be glad to do it."

Nell's eyes brightened. "How nice of you. Thanks."

William opened the door and stepped out on the porch to greet Nell. "Glad you could come on such short notice. Dr. Littleton is in the backyard."

William led Nell around the house following the brick walkway to the rear yard. The space was lush and green with borders of flowerbeds set around the edges of the property. To Nell, everything was a riot of color. The inn had a large stone patio, a fire pit, a garden swing, and tables and chairs placed here and there, some in the sun and others under the shade trees.

"Dr. Littleton arrived out of the blue about an hour ago," William said. "She's a friend of Pepper Forrest. She asked me a bunch of questions, most of which I couldn't answer. She has an appointment at the police department later today to speak with the investigators. I don't think she'll get much information from them. She's not a relative of Dr. Forrest so they won't share much of anything with her."

Nell nodded. "I think you're right. Did you learn anything about Dr. Littleton?"

"Not much. She lives in Boston, has been friends with Dr. Forrest for two years, works in the same department at the university in Boston. That's all she told me. Since you and your sister are trying to find out some things about the deceased woman, I thought I'd have you come down and have a chat with Dr. Littleton."

"I appreciate it," Nell said and as they turned into the backyard, she saw a woman sitting in a chair under the tall Maple tree.

William introduced Nell, and then headed inside to see to his guests.

Nell took the chair next to Dr. Littleton. "I'm very sorry about your friend."

Janis Littleton was in her late-thirties, had chin-length blond hair and big blue eyes, and looked athletic and fit. She seemed nervous and upset, touching her hair and passing her hand over her eyes, but was clearly trying to hide her feelings of distress. "I work in the same department that Pepper does ... did. I couldn't believe it when I heard the news. It's a terrible, terrible loss for the college community, but also for me personally. We were friends. I enjoyed her friendship immensely." The words caught in the woman's throat and she shook her head slowly.

"You came to Bluewater to speak with the police?" Nell asked.

"I hoped they could shed some light on what happened to Pepper."

"I'm sure they'll be eager to talk to you," Nell said even though she doubted the police would be keen to speak with Dr. Littleton.

"The innkeeper told me you were with Pepper right before she died," Janis said.

Nell corrected her. "I was working in the back-room of our shop. I only saw your friend from the back and only for a moment. My sister waited on her. Pepper purchased a necklace and then she left. I went into the front room to talk with my sister and I noticed a car speed away from the curb." She paused and swallowed. "The car hit your friend. We ran out to see if there was anything we could do, but it was too late. It happened very fast. Your friend didn't suffer." Nell tried to offer a bit of comfort.

Janis touched at her eyes with a tissue. "So it was definitely a hit and run?"

"It was. The car has been found. The driver hasn't been identified yet."

"How did Pepper seem when she was at your store?" Janis asked.

A shot of adrenaline raced through Nell. "She didn't shop for very long. She chose the necklace quickly, and as I said, I didn't interact with her at all. My sister didn't notice anything unusual. Pepper bought a necklace and left the shop. It was a brief interaction." Nell looked at Janis. "Why do you ask how Pepper seemed? Was anything wrong? Was anything going on with her?"

"No, at least I don't think so," Janis said. "I only wondered if she was in a hurry. Was she late for something? Did she rush into the street in her haste? I don't understand how someone could hit her in a town like this. People drive slowly in these little towns. There are tourists around. No one speeds down a street like that."

Except in this case, Nell thought, but didn't say the words out loud.

"I remember one odd thing." Janis squeezed her hands together. "When Pepper and I went out for a few drinks one night not long ago, she mentioned she felt she was being watched. Sometimes she had the impression she was being followed. I was worried and asked her some questions, but then she brushed it off saying she had an active imagination, that it was all foolishness. I didn't want to let it go, but she wouldn't say anymore."

Nell looked alarmed. "Do you think someone *was* following her?"

"I have no idea. I don't know why Pepper would think such a thing."

"What was Pepper like?" Nell asked.

Janis blinked in surprise, not expecting someone to ask her to describe her friend. "She was a nice person, great to be around, helpful, upbeat. She was quiet in a large group, but with a few friends, she was talkative and friendly. She easily put anyone at ease, you opened up to her, she was an excellent listener."

"You knew her for about two years?" Nell asked.

"That's right. She was very welcoming when I joined the department."

"Had anything been bothering her lately? Did she ever bring up being followed again?"

"No, she didn't." Janis tilted her head to the side in thought. "I don't think anything was bothering her. She gave no indication she was concerned about anything, but I can't say for sure."

"Was she married?"

A cloud settled over Janis's face. "She *was* married years ago. Her husband was killed in a car accident." The woman's shoulders slumped. "It happened about six months or so after they were married. What happened to Pepper is so unbelievable. About a year before her husband died, he and Pepper were in a serious car accident together. They were engaged at the time. It took months for them to recover from it. Then they got married, and her husband was killed in a crash. Now Pepper is dead from a car hitting her. It's like fate wouldn't stop until it took both of their lives."

A chill slipped over Nell's skin. It all seemed an impossible series of events.

"Did this all happen in Massachusetts?"

"No. Pepper and her husband lived in California. After he died, she moved to the Boston area."

"For a job?" Nell asked.

"No. She told me she moved here because it was as far away from her life in California as she could get without leaving the country. She was born in New Hampshire and her family moved to the West Coast when she was little."

"Was Pepper teaching at a university when she was married?"

"She was a high school chemistry teacher back then. She left the state because she was heartbroken over the loss of her husband and needed a huge change. Her first year in Massachusetts, she did odd jobs. She applied to do a Ph.D. and was accepted. When she finished the degree, she got a professorship at the university in Boston. That's where I met her."

"Are her parents still alive?" Nell asked.

"They passed away. Pepper was an only child. She told me she had no living relatives."

"Was she dating anyone recently?"

"No. She dated off and on, but could never find someone who was a good match," Janis said. "I always wondered if she wouldn't allow herself to get close to another man because of the loss she suffered. I really think she was trying to protect herself from being hurt again."

"Was there anyone she dated who maybe didn't like the fact that Pepper wouldn't commit to a relationship? Was there anyone she broke off with who was angry about being dropped?" Nell asked.

"I'm not really sure," Janis said, and then her eyes widened with a look of alarm. "Are you asking because ... do you think someone hurt Pepper deliberately?"

"I don't know anything," Nell said. "It crossed my mind that maybe someone had a grudge against Pepper, but from how you describe her, she sounds like a very caring person."

Janis didn't respond, she just looked across the yard, seemingly deep in thought. "I ... I'll have to think about this. I can't imagine someone being angry with Pepper. Everyone liked her. She was nice to everyone." Janis shook her head. "No, this had to be an accident."

Nell asked, "I understand Pepper came to Bluewater for a symposium. Did she also want a few days on her own?"

"It seemed to be a very spur of the moment thing." Janis held her hands tightly together in her lap. "Pepper texted me. She said she'd decided to take off for a couple of days to attend a symposium at the medical school in Bluewater. She said she'd see me on Monday."

"Did she do that from time to time?" Nell asked. "Did she go off for a couple of days on her own every now and then?"

"No. She never did. This was the first time. Honestly? I was very surprised she didn't ask me to go with her. We're in the same field. At first, I felt a little bad about it, but then I told myself that Pepper had been working hard and probably needed a change of scenery." Janis's face fell and her eyes teared up. "If I only she'd asked me to go along. Maybe she'd still be alive."

9

Nell and Dr. Rob decided to go for a run early in the morning when the air was cooler and the humidity was lower. When they returned to the university medical campus, they decided to sit on the outside patio to enjoy the glasses of lemonade they purchased in the cafeteria.

Rob asked Nell if there was any news related to the hit-and-run accident and she reported talking with William, the innkeeper at The Sandy Rose, about Pepper staying there. She also told him about seeing orange flashes in the windows of her house and on the street when returning home from town the other evening, and reported what she'd learned from, Pepper's friend, Dr. Janis Littleton.

"You've sure been busy," Rob said. "The neighbor saw someone lurking in your yard?"

"He thinks so. Iris and I thought we spotted someone in the shadows when we were getting closer to the house. I wouldn't have given it much thought if John and Ida hadn't seen something, too."

"You saw flashes of orange in the house?" Rob gave Nell a serious look.

With a nod, Nell said, "I didn't share that with John and Ida. The flashes were quick. At first, I worried the house was on fire, but when I looked again, they were gone. I saw a flash in the street. It shot into the air like a sparkler and the color disappeared. Was it a warning of some kind? *Was* someone looking around our house?"

"It's possible that you're picking up on energy like you did when you saw Pepper Forrest in the shop," Rob said. "If someone was in your yard checking out the house, the person could have left behind traces of his intention. You picked up on it and saw it as orange flashes."

Nell had a skeptical expression on her face. "Really? Do you really think it's possible for people to see energy that's given off by others?"

"If you asked the average person if it was possible for someone to see millions more colors in the world than they were able to see, they'd most likely say no," Rob said.

Nell cocked her head to the side. "But I'm asking this question of an expert who studies vision and energy and the structure of the eye. I'm not asking an average person, so I don't expect an average answer. Do *you* think it's possible?"

"That was my point." When Rob lifted the tall glass of lemonade, the ice cubes clinked against the sides. "Because something is unusual, it is often distrusted or dismissed. I do think it's possible that people's emotions can become energy and that it might be possible to see that energy. By some people."

Dr. Atkins Murray approached the table and sat down before Nell could ask Rob another question. "I was looking for you."

"Hello to you, too," Rob kidded the man for his abrupt appearance at their table.

"Oh, hello," Atkins said and then glanced at Nell, nodded, and said a quick hello to her. "I have some articles I want to discuss," he told Rob.

Rob said, "Nell and I just finished a run. Why don't you get a cold drink and sit with us for a while? We can go over the articles once I'm back in my office."

Atkins face showed impatience. "I don't want a drink."

"Well, you can sit and chat with us while we finish up. We won't be long."

Nell felt a little surge of annoyance. She'd wanted to talk privately with Rob about what she'd been experiencing, and now that Atkins had taken a seat, she wouldn't be able to pick Rob's brain.

Rob tried to make small talk that included Atkins. "Nell and I were discussing the hit-and-run accident that happened a few days ago."

Atkins grunted. "She should have watched out for cars on the street."

Nell's face flushed with a jolt of anger. "I saw the speeding car. If you'd started to walk across the street, it would have hit you. There wasn't anything Dr. Forrest could have done to avoid it. There wasn't any time for her to react. That's how fast the vehicle was going."

Atkins stared at Nell. "You were there?"

"Yes."

"You saw it?"

"I saw the car speed by. I was inside my store. I didn't see the actual impact, but I heard it."

"I knew her," Atkins said.

Nell's eyes widened with surprise. "Who? Pepper Forrest?"

"I met her in Boston when we were both working at the same university."

"Did you know her well?" Nell asked, amazed that Atkins knew the woman, but didn't show any shock or concern that she'd been killed.

"Not that well."

"You only met her once?" Rob asked.

"More than once. We dated."

Nell almost fell out of her chair. "You dated? For how long?"

"A handful of times." Atkins looked off across the campus lawn.

"What does a handful mean?" Nell asked. "Five times? Twenty times?"

The new researcher turned to Nell. "I didn't keep track of the exact number of times we went out."

Nell took a breath and when she spoke again, she made sure her tone sounded interested instead of accusatory. "Why did you stop seeing Pepper after only a handful of dates?"

"She didn't wish to continue the relationship," Atkins said.

"Did she say why?" Rob asked.

"I don't recall." Atkins sounded grumpy.

"What do you know about Dr. Forrest?" Nell questioned, hoping to learn more about the woman.

Atkins straightened in his seat. "I don't engage in gossip."

"It's only conversation about the woman," Rob explained. "No one wishes to gossip about her. We'd only like to know what she was like."

Nell didn't want the conversation to change direction that fast. "Is there something to gossip about? Did something happen that made people talk?"

"I don't wish to speak ill of the woman," Atkins said.

"Did she do something wrong?" Nell asked, wishing the researcher would be more forthcoming.

"She broke off with me." Atkins looked at Nell like she was thick-headed.

"Can you tell us about Pepper?" Rob asked. "What was she like?"

"She was smart, attractive, well-spoken. She was interesting to talk with, she knew a lot about varied subjects." Atkins's face looked stony.

"Do you know anything about her background?" Rob asked.

"She lived in California. Her husband died suddenly. She didn't have any family. I believe she worked briefly as a high school teacher. She left the West Coast to study in the Boston area and after she finished, she worked at a university in the city."

"How long ago did you date?" Nell asked the man.

"A year."

Nell continued with her questions. "Did Pepper ever mention being worried or frightened about anything? Or anyone?"

Atkins's blue eyes bored into Nell's. "No. What in the world could she have been frightened of?"

Nell made some suggestions. "An ex-boyfriend who was bothering her. A student who didn't like his grade. Someone on the university campus who had a run-in with her. Someone who lived nearby. Did Pepper ever confide in you about anything odd or unusual that might have happened to her?"

"No, she didn't. I don't remember anything like that," Atkins said.

"I heard Pepper had been in a serious car accident when she lived in California," Nell said. "Did she tell you anything about that?"

"No." Atkins appeared to become more unsettled as the conversation went on.

"Had you been in contact with Pepper since you and she stopped dating?" Rob asked.

"Not at all. Our offices were on different sides of the campus. We didn't run into each other. I left Boston to take this position."

Something picked at Nell. "Did Pepper know you were working in Bluewater?"

"I have no idea. I certainly didn't tell her."

Nell leaned forward. "Did you happen to see her in town while she was visiting here?"

"I did not." Atkins's voice was stern.

"I'm sorry if speaking about Pepper is upsetting to you," Nell said. "We only wondered what she was like. I apologize for bringing it up."

Atkins shifted uncomfortably in his seat. "I don't have any desire to talk about Pepper. I wasn't pleased when she wouldn't see me anymore. I don't mean to sound cruel, but I really don't have any interest in what happened. Pepper became a stranger to me." The researcher stood. "Now, if you'll excuse me, I need to get back to work." He looked at Rob. "Let me know when you're back in your office." Atkins strode away from the patio.

"He sure got annoyed talking about Dr. Forrest." Rob watched his co-worker hurry away.

When Nell didn't say anything, Rob turned his attention to her. "What's wrong?"

Nell swallowed hard. "At the end of the conversation, Atkins started to take on a color."

"What did you see?" Rob asked quietly.

Nell's voice was almost inaudible. "Red. Atkins was covered in red. Just like Pepper was."

Rob's eyebrows shot up. "Do you sense that Atkins is in danger?"

"No." Nell shook her head. "I feel anger from him. It feels like rage."

Rob looked to be sure the researcher was in the distance and out of earshot. "He was very bothered that Dr. Forrest wouldn't go out with him after the first dates they had together. He seems to be harboring resentment about it."

"How resentful is he?" Nell asked.

Rob understood what his friend was getting at. "Not Atkins. He's odd, sure, but he wouldn't hurt anyone."

"How long have you known him?" Nell asked.

Rob let out a sigh. "Not long."

Nell shivered, not wanting to believe it was possible she'd been sitting with Pepper's killer. "Where was Atkins on the day Pepper was killed? Was he in the office at the time she was hit? Do you remember if he was here?"

"I wasn't here that afternoon," Rob said. "I was in a meeting in Boston."

"Oh. Can you find out from someone if Atkins was here?"

Rob gave a quick nod. "I'll ask around. Discreetly."

10

"See, right here. And here, too. These posts are rotting." Violet had a screwdriver in her hand and was poking the tip into the soft wood of the deck and the posts that held it up. "It needs to be replaced or we're going to step outside one of these days and fall through the floor."

Iris sat in the grass listening to the two sisters discuss the needed reconstruction. She woofed when Violet mentioned falling through the deck floor.

"How much will it cost?" Nell asked while peering at the underside of the wide porch.

"Plenty," Violet said. "We need to replace it with that recycled material, composite-type stuff so it won't rot like this again."

"Will it cost a lot?"

Violet shrugged. "Thousands."

"Really?" Nell groaned. "Should we just knock it down and not have a deck?"

"But we use it all the time." Violet stuck the screwdriver into the pocket of her shorts. "We can see the ocean from the deck. Wouldn't you miss it?"

"I would, but I might miss the money that gets taken out of my savings account more."

John Patrick, the neighbor, came into the yard and Iris trotted over to greet him.

"Hi, John," Nell said.

"What's going on? Why are you under the deck?" The older man patted the dog on the head and Iris was lapping it up.

"It's rotting," Nell explained. "It either has to be replaced or it has to be torn down."

"What are you going to do?" John stroked his chin.

"We were discussing the cost. We're not sure what to do."

"A deck can be a nice selling point for a house," John said as he checked the posts for the rot.

"But we aren't going to sell it," Violet told their neighbor.

"I'm glad to hear that. We'd miss you two. It'd be

a shame to take it down. You've got such a nice view from the deck." John adjusted his eyeglasses. "Have you met the handyman-gardener who works at The Sandy Rose? His name's Bobby. He's done some work for us. He does a good job and he's very reasonable in what he charges. Why don't you ask him for a quote?"

"I talked to Bobby the other day," Nell said. "He seems like a nice guy. He offered to come over sometime and give us some advice on how to improve the gardens back here. Mom had a green thumb. I think it's pretty clear that we don't."

"It looks fine," John said.

"*Fine* was a word you could use to describe Mom's gardens," Violet smiled. "We're not living up to it."

"Take Bobby up on his offer to check out the gardens," John suggested. "He can replace the deck and get the flowers back into shape."

"I'll talk to him," Nell said.

"Ida sent me over to invite you to dinner. It's our turn. How about Thursday?" John asked. Since Violet and Nell had moved into the Bluewater house, they'd been taking turns with John and Ida hosting dinners for each other at least once a month. After the meal, the four of them would play a board game together while Iris slept on a rug.

"Thursday's great," Violet said. "We'll bring some wine."

When John returned to his house, Violet said to her sister, "I have something to tell you. Peter was here this morning. They're having trouble with Pepper Forrest's case. There's a lot of pressure on the department to get this thing solved, but every bit of information they follow turns into a dead end."

Nell said, "I hope something works out soon and they can find the killer."

Violet stared at Nell.

"What?" Nell began to feel uneasy. "Why are you looking at me that way?"

"Dani and Peter came by earlier to talk to you, but you weren't here. Peter had a meeting with Chief Lambert. The chief told Peter he'd been talking with the Sweet Cove Chief of Police, Phillip Martin."

"Does Chief Martin have a lead?" Nell's face took on a hopeful expression.

"Not necessarily," Violet said. "Not the way you think."

Nell tilted her head to the side. "What do you mean?"

"Chief Martin told Chief Lambert that he sometimes works with a psychic or an intuit who brings an important and invaluable viewpoint to difficult cases."

Suddenly, Nell's eyes darkened. "Wait a minute...."

"Chief Lambert knows you're a tetrachromat."

Nell's voice was soft. "Did Peter tell him what I saw the day Pepper was in the store? Did he tell the chief that I saw red all over Pepper Forrest?"

Violet didn't say anything.

"Did he?" Nell pressed.

"He might have mentioned something about what you saw."

"Oh, no," Nell groaned and began to pace around the yard, her auburn ponytail bobbing with every step. "The chief is going to think I'm a freak."

"Peter thinks you can be of help," Violet said. "You told me yourself you wanted to do something to help the case, to help Pepper. You said if this thing of yours is some new skill, then you want to use it to help others."

Nell stopped pacing. "What if it won't work when I need it to? What if I only see the colors on someone whenever the mood strikes? I'll be good for nothing. I'll be useless. I'll let everyone down."

Violet smiled. "No, you won't. Peter told the chief

that this is new. That you don't understand it and that you're talking to Dr. Rob about trying to figure it out."

"What did the chief say?" Nell asked warily.

"Chief Lambert was friendly with Mom and Dad. He knows us. He was amazed that you saw the red. Peter said they could sure use some help on the case. The chief wants to talk to you."

"Oh, gosh." Nell's voice shook and she ran her hand nervously over the top of her hair.

"Peter will be there with you. It will be just the three of you. No one else will sit in on the meeting," Violet said. "I'll go, too, if you want me to."

"Oh, gosh," Nell said again. She sank down onto the grass and Iris rushed over to lick her face.

Violet sat next to her sister. "You could go and talk to the chief. Listen to what he has to say. If you feel uncomfortable about it, then decline whatever it is he's going to ask of you. Chief Lambert is a nice man. He won't push you to do something you don't want to do."

"Okay." Nell nodded. "I'll talk to him, but I'm not making any promises."

Violet, Nell, Chief Alan Lambert, and Peter sat around the wooden conference table in an office of the Bluewater Police Department. Chief Lambert was in his mid-sixties and had bright blue eyes and a bald head. He was still in shape, but remaining fit took him more work than it ever had in the past.

The chief cleared his throat and thanked the sisters for coming in. "Peter tells me you had quite an experience. Would you mind telling me about what happened the afternoon that Dr. Forrest suffered the accident?"

Nell sipped from the glass of water that sat on the table in front of her. Her heart pounded like a sledgehammer and a faint bit of perspiration showed on her forehead. After taking a look at her sister and receiving an encouraging nod from Violet, Nell told her story.

"Amazing." Chief Lambert was intrigued and fascinated by what Nell had experienced. "Have you ever had this happen to you prior to that day?"

"Never. Nothing like it had ever happened to me before."

"Has it happened again since Dr. Forrest's accident?" the chief asked.

A tightness gathered in Nell's stomach as she thought of Atkins Murray and how she saw him

covered in red when she and Rob talked to him
about his relationship with Pepper. Not wanting to
implicate the man, she didn't mention what she saw.
If Rob discovered Atkins wasn't in the office or lab
on the afternoon of the hit-and-run, then she would
share that information with Chief Lambert.

"I was walking home the other night with Iris. I
saw orange flashes in the windows of our house, and
I thought I saw someone in the shadows in our yard.
The neighbor saw someone in our yard, too, when
he happened to look out his window. I also saw a
flash of orange in the street when I was going into
the house. I think it was a warning of some kind."
Nell told the chief Dr. Rob's theory about emotions
being expressed as visible energy that she was able
to pick up on.

"It's quite a theory. Incredible, really." Chief
Lambert picked up his pen and held it in his hand,
rolling it between his fingers. "Peter must have told
you I've been in contact with some other depart-
ments in the area. Several have good working rela-
tionships with a few people who have some unique
abilities. The other chiefs aren't willing to share
those people's names. Most of those psychics, if
that's what you call them, have requested anonymity

and will only work with the chiefs they feel comfortable with."

"We're up a tree here," Peter said to Nell. "We're running into brick walls. Dr. Forrest had registered for a symposium at the medical school, but she never checked in. She didn't attend the lectures. Why didn't she?" He held Nell's eyes. "We could use some help. I told Chief Lambert this ability is new to you, that you don't know how to control it, or what to expect from it."

The chief said, "I'm willing to take the opportunity. I'm willing to see if what you experienced could help us with this case. Of course, your work with us will be held in confidence. You'll be anonymous. I'll even have papers drawn up spelling all of this out." Chief Lambert put his pen down and leaned slightly forward, his blue eyes focused on Nell. "Will you give this a try? Will you see if you can help the case? Will you trust us to keep your involvement in confidence?"

"What kinds of things would you want me to do?" Nell asked, her voice shaking a little.

Chief Lambert said, "I might ask you to talk to some people. I'd go over the questions I'd want you to ask beforehand. I'd probably ask you to visit a few places. Peter would go with you. I promise I will never put you in a dangerous situation. If you don't want to do something, just say the word. You can back out any time you want. I've never worked with anyone with sensitive abilities." The corners of the chief's mouth turned up. "I guess we'll be learning together."

"What do you say, Nell?" Peter asked.

Nell made eye contact with Violet, and then she turned to the chief and said, "Okay. Let's give it a try."

11

Nell's first assignment for the police department would be to accompany Peter to the car rental place where the vehicle that hit Pepper had been leased. Officers had already interviewed the employee who did the paperwork with the driver, but another visit wouldn't hurt and Chief Lambert was hopeful Nell would be able to pick up on something they'd overlooked.

Walking into the center of town on her way to the police department to meet Peter, Nell received a text from him saying he was running late and would she mind passing some time at Dani's coffee shop where he'd pick her up in thirty minutes.

Nell was happy to see an empty table by the

window where she'd be able to see Peter pull up to the curb.

Dani stood behind the counter and when she saw Nell enter, she raised an empty coffee mug with a questioning look.

Nell smiled and nodded, and then took a seat at the table, and in less than three minutes, Dani had set down a hot cup of coffee for her friend.

"Why aren't you at the shop?" Dani asked.

"I'm meeting Peter in a little while." Nell made eye contact with the coffee shop owner.

"Ah." Dani gave a knowing nod of her head. "Hopefully something useful will come out of the meeting." After a little conversation, Dani had to return to handle the takeout customers.

As Nell poured some milk into her coffee, she noticed someone standing next to her and looked up to see Detective Michael Gregory, the law enforcement officer who had come up from Boston to assist on the case.

"May I?" The detective gestured to the empty seat at the table and Nell, feeling a flush of warmth in her cheeks, nodded.

The detective introduced himself. "I saw you on the deck at the restaurant a few days ago. You were with Dani and another woman."

"That was my sister, Violet." Nell's heart pounded hard from her proximity to the detective and she mentally chided herself for acting like a schoolgirl fawning over a good-looking man.

"I saw you at the police station. You had a meeting with Chief Lambert." The way the detective's dark brown eyes searched Nell's face made her uncomfortable.

"I did meet with him." She lifted her mug to her lips as a way of defending her space.

"What did you talk about?" Detective Gregory asked after one of the employees delivered a black coffee to the man.

Nell steadied herself. She didn't like the detective's fishing for information so she gave him a pleasant smile. "Did you ask the chief what we talked about?"

"I haven't had a chance."

"Well, I bet you will soon. You must be at the station pretty often."

The detective silently admired the way Nell was being evasive. "Since we're sharing a table, you can save me some time by sharing what you discussed with the chief."

"Why do you need to know?" Nell asked. "We just had a casual chat."

"Casual? You mean about the weather?"

"A little about the weather." Nell had no intention of explaining her visit to Chief Lambert.

The detective asked a different question. "You'd met Pepper Forrest?"

The sudden inquiry took Nell by surprise and she shifted around in her chair. "No, I hadn't. She'd been in our store, but I was working in the studio in the backroom. I saw Pepper from the back, but I didn't have any interaction with her. My sister waited on her."

"She made a purchase from your shop?"

"She bought a necklace. My sister rang up the sale. Pepper left right after that."

"Did you see her get hit by the car?" Detective Gregory asked.

Nell's breath caught in her throat for a second. "I did not. I did see the car speed away from the curb and down the street. I've told two officers all of this when they interviewed me."

"It doesn't hurt to discuss it again," the detective said.

"I suppose not." Nell glanced out the window hoping to see Peter's car pull up.

"What kind of a car did you see speeding down the street?"

"A small sedan."

"What color was it?"

Nell saw a black car, but she knew the witnesses had reported a white vehicle hitting Pepper, so she decided to align her answer with what others had told police. "It was a light-colored car."

"Are you sure?" The detective stared at Nell.

"It was light-colored, yes. White, cream, a white-gray, something like that. It sped past the store window very fast."

"I see." Detective Gregory took a swallow from his cup. "I understand you're an artist."

"That's right. I sell my work online and at the store. I do private commissions, as well. I also do some graphic design work on a contract by contract basis."

"You must be very busy."

"Busy enough."

"Have you lived in Bluewater all of your life?"

"My sister and I grew up in central Massachusetts. My mother inherited a house here and we used it in summers and on weekends. When my parents passed away, my sister and I decided to move into the house here and make Bluewater our home."

"How long ago did you move here permanently?"

"About seven or eight months ago. It's not a big

move for us. The family had the house since before we were born. It feels like home," Nell said.

Although Nell was uncomfortable being interrogated by the detective, when he gave her a warm smile, it sent shivers down to her toes. Annoyed by the effect he had on her, she attempted to deflect it by picking up her phone to check for a message from Peter.

"I need to go outside. I'm meeting someone." Nell gathered her things and stood up. "Have a good day," she said as she left the coffee house.

As soon as she was on the sidewalk, Peter pulled up and she got in. She spotted the detective watching them as Peter maneuvered the car into the Main Street traffic and drove away.

ON THE WAY to the car rental company, Nell reviewed some photographs from the security camera located above the rental place's customer counter. The pictures showed a man signing a form, handing over his license to be copied, and being given the keys to the car. The picture was grainy and snowy and didn't give much of a picture of the man leasing the vehicle.

"Are these helpful to you?" Nell asked as she squinted and held the photos closer to her eyes. "I can't even make out the man's face."

"It's not much help, but we can see the general height and weight of the guy. We can see that he's right-handed. He's most likely wearing a wig, and he's got those sunglasses on so that impairs our ability to see his facial characteristics and what his hair is really like. But it's better than nothing."

"It's thought the man used a fake license and fake credit card to rent the car?" Nell asked.

"Yes. Someone forged the license and the credit card was obtained from stolen information from a deceased person."

"People do that? Steal dead people's information?" Nell looked aghast.

"All the time." Peter sighed as he pulled into a parking lot and stopped. "Here we are. The man we're going in to see is Sam Willins. He did the paperwork with the guy who rented the vehicle. What he told us isn't that helpful. It was a normal transaction. Nothing stood out. Chief Lambert just wants you to look around, listen as I talk to Sam. See if you pick up on anything."

Nell said skeptically, "Okay, but any energy that was given off on the day of the rental has long since dissipated. There won't be anything left in there for me to see."

"That's all right," Peter said. "Being here is a way to get you familiar with the case so don't be concerned if you don't see anything."

Reassured, Nell walked with Peter to the building.

Peter greeted Sam Willins and the three of them sat at a small table in a corner of the room.

"Thanks for speaking with me again," Peter said to Sam and he introduced Nell. "This is Ellen Finley. She's helping on the case."

Sam was in his late fifties, was slightly over-weight, and had buzzed brown hair and brown eyes that looked a little bloodshot. He shook hands politely with Nell.

"Can you describe the man who rented the car again? I know you've done it several times already, but it will benefit Ms. Finley to hear it straight from you," Peter said.

Sam cleared his throat. "He seemed like a normal guy. We had the paperwork ready and the car was parked in the side lot for pickup. He had longer hair, down to his chin, dark, a little scruffy. He had on sunglasses so I couldn't see his eye color, but I wouldn't have noticed anyway. He was about five-foot, ten or eleven. He was thin, but I got the feeling he worked out. He looked sort of muscular, but not overboard or anything. Just strong for his build, not soft like me." Sam patted his belly.

Peter asked more questions and Sam responded like he'd answered them many times.

"What color skin did he have?" Nell asked.

"Medium."

"Any tattoos or scars or anything like that?"

"Nothing I noticed."

"What about his hands and his fingers? Were his fingernails dirty? Did his hands look like he did hard work?"

Sam's face scrunched up in thought. "I'm not sure about that."

"What was his voice like?" Nell asked.

"I don't know what you mean." Sam looked confused.

"Deep? High-pitched? An accent?"

"Normal. A normal guy's voice," Sam replied.

"Did he seem nervous?"

"No. He didn't seem nervous to me. He was in and out of here quick."

"Can you show me where he was standing when he was signing the papers?" Nell asked.

"Oh. Sure." Sam got to his feet and led Nell to the

counter. "He was standing about here. I was behind the counter."

Nell looked down at the surface of the countertop trying to pick up on any energy left behind by Pepper's killer. She moved her gaze around the back of the counter and then around the room and towards the glass door that led outside. When she turned back, she slowly ran her hand over the top of the counter, and for a quick moment, something seemed to flicker in her vision, but it was gone before she knew what it was. "Thank you," she told Sam. "Peter told me you're always a big help."

Sam beamed at the compliment. "Come back anytime. I'm glad to do what I can."

Back in the car, Peter asked, "Nothing, huh?"

Nell recalled the tiny flicker of something she'd experienced while standing at the counter. It picked at her, but not knowing how to describe it, she said only, "I guess not."

12

————

The sweet scent of rosa rugosa drifted on the air to where Nell and Violet were pulling weeds from the flowerbeds along the public walkway that meandered over the rocks and cliffs along the ocean. The sisters volunteered once a week with a group that tended and maintained the two-mile walkway, planting and caring for the flowers and ground cover, pulling weeds, and keeping the cement staircases leading down to the beach safe and clean.

The sun beat down on the volunteers as they spread out along the path with gardening tools, wheelbarrows, flowers in small containers, and bags of mulch.

"I'm glad I brought my hat today." Violet lifted

the brimmed, straw hat from her head and brushed away the beads of perspiration on her forehead. "I wasn't expecting it to be so hot."

"It's early for the heat to be lingering." Nell lifted the bottom of her t-shirt and flapped it a little trying to create a breeze to cool her skin. "And it's darned humid." Looking down at the white sand beach at the bottom of the stairs, she admired the riot of colors in the sand and in the water. The sun always made everything shimmer with millions of hues, and the beauty of it made Nell wish that Violet could see what she experienced. A few big waves crashed against the beach and Nell said, "I'd love to peel these sweaty, wet clothes off and go jump in the ocean."

"I'll be right behind you if you do." Violet chuckled imagining everyone's shock when two women ran by in their underwear on the way into the waves.

Nell pulled her auburn locks into a high ponytail to get it off of her neck and then applied sunscreen to her neck and shoulders.

An older volunteer came up to them pushing a wheelbarrow full of flowers. With a hearty hello, Ben said, "Lucy says these are the ones that are going in by the benches. Do you need a shovel?"

"We've got a couple." Nell smiled and thanked the man for bringing them the blooms.

"A couple of new volunteers are going to join you in a few minutes. You'll show them the ropes?" Ben asked.

"We'll be glad to," Violet said.

"Okay, then. Text me if you need anything," Ben told them cheerfully as he headed back along the walkway.

The two-mile path along the scenic cliffs started in the center of Bluewater Cove and ended up in a park down near the harbor after passing by spectacular views and vistas. The path was popular and well-traveled by both tourists and townspeople as well as by early-morning joggers.

Nell took the flats of flowers and placed them here and there in the beds near the benches to see how they looked. She stepped back, then moved a few of them around while Violet carried over two bags of the mulch.

"Rob called me," Nell said. "He told me no one can remember if Atkins Murray was in the office or lab on the afternoon Pepper was hit by the car. Everyone was coming and going. Some of the researchers were in meetings, some went to a short lecture by a visiting professor. No one can recall if Atkins was present at any of the gatherings."

"Too bad." Violet's face fell at the news. "Should we tell Chief Lambert that Atkins dated Pepper and she broke off the relationship?"

"I think we should. The chief may know already, but I'd feel better if we spoke to him about it in case it's new information. I should also tell him that I saw red covering Atkins when we talked on the patio at the university." Nell gave a little shiver of worry. "I hope he has an alibi for where he was that afternoon. I hate to think he's the one that hurt Pepper."

"It would come as a surprise to Rob to think he's been working with a murderer," Violet noted. With a sad shrug, she added, "I guess people can surprise you sometimes."

Nell picked up the spade and dug a small hole to plant one of the flowers in.

Violet asked, "Has Rob told you what sort of experiments he wants to do with you to evaluate your ability to pick up on people's emotions by seeing colors in the energy they're giving off?"

Nell glanced around to be sure no one was listening to their conversation. "He's doing research on it, then he'll design the experiment. The difficulty will come in figuring out how I'll receive the stimuli.

I need someone who is giving off strong emotion. Rob is unsure how he'll manage that."

"He'll have to haul you around the university looking for people who are having fights or arguments or who are really angry about something," Violet smiled. "It won't be easy."

"It seems impossible to control the experiment," Nell admitted. "If we can't do the evaluation, it will be just fine by me."

Two women approached and greeted the sisters. "I'm Willa." One of them extended her hand.

"I'm Susan," the other one said. "Nice to meet you. It's our first time volunteering."

Nell thanked them for helping out and explained the day's tasks showing them where the flowers were to be positioned, where to get fresh water, and how to place the mulch when a section had been completed. She and Willa paired up and Violet and Susan took a wheelbarrow and some tools and headed further down the walkway to work on a separate bed of flowers.

Nell and the new volunteer chatted while they worked. Willa, about thirty years old, had short blond hair and blue eyes. "I live one town over. My husband and I take the kids here all the time to go to the beach. We love the restaurants, too, and walking around town and along this cliff walk. I've wanted to volunteer for a few years and never got around to it. Finally, here I am."

"We're glad to have you," Nell told the young woman. "Many hands make light work."

"My husband and I use that saying around the house all the time. It's so true." Willa patted some soil around a newly-planted bunch of pink impatiens. "Wasn't it awful about the woman who was visiting and got hit by that car? And the guy didn't even stop to help or to call an ambulance." Willa shook her head. "What kind of person would do such a thing?"

"He must have panicked," Nell suggested.

"Maybe. But wouldn't your panic subside and then you'd think it best to call the police?"

"He might be terrified now because he drove away after hitting her."

Willa sat back on her heels with a trowel in one hand and a bunch of impatiens in the other. "Do you think this guy might have hit her on purpose?"

Nell made eye contact with the woman. "Why do you think so?"

"Do you know anything about Pepper Forrest?" Willa asked.

Nell didn't want to share that she had been asked

to help the police with the case. "Only what I've read in the news or heard on television." A thought popped into her head. "Did you know her?"

"No, I didn't, but she called our office and asked for an appointment. I spoke to her on the phone. It creeps me out that I spoke with her one day, and then the next day, she was dead."

Nell's heart began to race. "What kind of office do you work in?"

"I'm the office manager. I work for three private investigators," Willa said.

Nell almost tipped over onto her butt. "Private investigators?"

"The office is in Bluewater City, about fifteen minutes from the Cove. Dr. Forrest called the day before she was hit by the car. I made an appointment for her for the day after she died. It's horrible."

"Did she say what she wanted investigated?" Nell asked.

"She said she was looking for someone and needed help locating the person. She was worried that she was being followed. She told me she attended a talk in Boston about personal safety given by one of our PIs a couple of months ago. That's how she knew about our office. I asked a few questions so I could assign the right investigator to her case, but she wouldn't tell me anything more. That's not unusual though. Lots of clients only want to speak with the investigator. They want things to be as private as possible."

"Was that the only time you spoke with Dr. Forrest?" Nell questioned.

"Just the one time." Willa began to dig a few more holes. "I can't stop thinking about it. She said she wanted someone found. She sounded concerned for her safety." Willa paused and looked at Nell with narrowed eyes. "Did the person she wanted found, find her first?"

Nell's blood went cold. "Did you tell the police Pepper Forrest made an appointment to speak with an investigator?"

"I didn't. I heard she had died and I deleted the appointment in our online system," Willa said.

"Did you tell the investigator one of his or her appointments had been hit by a car?" Nell asked.

"I did tell him. He was surprised by it, but not overly so. He hadn't met with her yet."

"Did you or the investigator notify the police?"

Willa's eyes widened at the question. "It was an accident. Why would we tell the police?"

"You said you wondered if the driver hit her deliberately," Nell pointed out.

"I was just talking. I don't really think it happened on purpose." Willa stared at Nell.

Violet walked up the path towards them. "Lucy texted us. She asked if Susan and Willa could meet her at the end of the cliff walk to help her with a different project."

"At the town end or where it ends in the park?" Willa shook some soil from her hands.

"The park end," Violet clarified.

"Thanks for helping," Nell told the woman. "I'm sure we'll work together soon."

When Willa headed towards the park, Nell told her sister what she'd learned about Pepper making an appointment with a private investigator.

"Do you think she knew she was in danger?" Violet asked.

"It's possible, isn't it? Dr. Forrest called an office of private investigators located in Bluewater. She lived in Boston so why wouldn't she call an investigator in Boston to help her with whatever it was she needed done? Why did she have to call the office of a PI she'd heard give a talk?"

Violet said, "Because she wanted to be sure *someone* didn't find out what she was doing."

"Exactly," Nell agreed.

13

Nell walked around to the back of The Sandy Rose inn to the outbuilding where the innkeeper told Nell she could find Bobby, the gardener and handyman. Bobby had paid a visit to Nell's and Violet's house to take a look at their gardens and to inspect the deck and its supporting columns. He gave some advice about how to help the flowers flourish and discussed what would be involved in repairing and shoring up the deck. He wrote up his proposal and an estimate and left it with the sisters to consider whether or not they wanted to make the repairs or preferred to have the deck removed.

After much talk about the cost and if they should spend the money, they decided to go ahead with fixing the deck because they knew they would miss sitting out there enjoying the beautiful views.

Nell decided to drop off the contract and the deposit check on the way to see a new client who was commissioning a painting of a ship at sea.

Following the short path past some trees and shrubs, Nell came to the two outbuildings, one was a small cottage the handyman was given rent-free as partial payment for his services. The other was a large shed Bobby used as a workshop.

Approaching the door of the shed, Nell heard the sound of a buzzing saw and smelled the scent of cut wood. Bobby stood at a work table running a handheld saw.

Nell waited until he was finished before saying hello.

Bobby turned around with an expectant look and smiled when he saw who was at the door. "Come in. This is the woodworking shop. When I first started working here, the shed was empty and William told me I could use it for my hobby."

Nell glanced around at the wooden items Bobby had created or was in the middle of working on ... wine racks, book shelves, bird houses, dressers.

"Wow. Your things are wonderful." Nell ran her hand over the top of a dresser. "So finely crafted."

Bobby had a big smile on his face as he showed Nell some of his most recent pieces. "I bring them into shops in the area to sell on commission. I also take special orders from people. I do small things, too. Salad bowls, cutting boards, things like that. I even make pens." He removed one from his shirt pocket to show Nell who admired the fine workmanship and the multiple colors running through the wood. She knew Bobby couldn't see all the colors so she didn't mention them when she praised the man for his expert work.

"I've been woodworking since I was a little kid. I love working with wood and using my vision to make something beautiful and useful." Bobby lovingly ran his hand over the top of a wine rack.

"You have quite a few talents," Nell said. "Gardening, woodworking, all-round-handyman."

"You'll notice they all involve working with my hands. I couldn't stand sitting at a desk all day. That would drive me bonkers. I need to move around, be outside. I need to be building or fixing things, creating something. I'm lucky I found things I like to do and can make a living at them."

"How long have you worked for William here at the inn?" Nell asked.

"Oh, let's see. I started in January so almost six months."

"Where did you work before that? Have you always worked at inns?"

"Here and there, up and down the coast. I like it here though. I get the free cottage to live in, a decent wage. William is easy to work for and he lets me use the shed for my woodworking shop. I don't like winter much, but I work in the shop and there's always a lot to do here at the inn so before I knew it, it was spring again."

Nell nodded, and then asked, "Did you meet Pepper Forrest when she was here?"

A look of confusion showed on Bobby's face. "Who? Oh, the woman who died recently?"

"She was staying here at the inn. I wondered if you'd bumped into her while you were working."

"If I did, I don't remember her. She didn't look familiar to me when I saw her photo on the news. The guests come and go. Most only stay two or three nights." Bobby asked, "Why do you ask about her?"

Nell brushed off the question. "No reason. I just wondered how she seemed."

"Seemed? How do you mean?"

"I wondered if something might have been bothering her."

"Why do you think that?" Bobby looked interested. "She was on vacation, wasn't she?"

"She was here to attend a symposium at the medical school. William said she'd booked a few nights here at the inn."

"I don't see why anything would be bothering someone when they're just going to listen to some talks."

"Yeah." Nell smiled and handed some papers to Bobby. "Anyway, we signed the contract for the deck, and here's a deposit check."

"Great. I can get started in a day or two. Like I said, my main job is here at The Sandy Rose so I have to fit in the secondary jobs around that. I won't be working at your house every day, but I will get the deck done in a timely manner." Bobby took his handmade pen out, signed one of the copies, made a note on it that he'd received the deposit, and handed it back to Nell. "It will look terrific when I'm done and it will last for a long time. Guaranteed."

NELL, Violet, and John and Ida Patrick sat around their deck table under a star-filled night sky enjoying a dinner of calzones, salad, and spaghetti.

Iris rested on the deck watching the fireflies sparkle on and off as they darted around the yard. The heat of the day had left behind a warm, pleasant evening with a gentle breeze coming off the ocean that pushed away the humidity.

"What a perfect night," Violet said as she lifted her wine glass to her lips.

"And what a perfect meal," Nell told the couple. "Everything is delicious."

"Ida is the best cook," John said proudly as he smiled at his wife of fifty years.

"John is being too flattering. He's the one who made the calzones ... with his secret recipe," Ida told them with a wink.

Nell and Violet reported they'd made a decision about their deck and had hired Bobby, the inn's handyman to do the job.

"He does excellent work. He can be focused and quiet at times so don't feel like he's being sullen towards you."

Nell was surprised to hear this. "He was nothing but personable when he came to give us an estimate and when I saw him this morning when I dropped off the paperwork."

"Bobby swings between being charming and pleasant, and moody and sour. It's his personality.

Don't take it personally," John said. "It never affects the quality of his work."

The sisters were glad John shared the information with them.

"I would have thought he was angry with something we'd done or said," Violet told the couple.

The conversation moved from one topic to another, and then Ida said, "The police still haven't found that hit-and-run driver. It's a shame someone can kill another person, take off, and not have to face the consequences of his actions."

"They'll find him one of these days," John said, pouring more wine into the glasses.

Although the Patricks were aware that Nell was a tetrachromat, she hadn't spoken to them about seeing Pepper Forrest shaded in red on the afternoon of the accident. Having known and trusted the couple for years, she decided to share her experience with them.

When the details had been explained, John and Ida took the tale in stride.

"It's nothing more than an expansion of your already special abilities," Ida told Nell.

"It's plain that you were able to pick up on the woman's emotions in a visual way," John said. "It is amazing to people like us because we don't share the capability, but as you and Violet said yourselves, the incredible things people have accomplished or developed in recent years would have been considered impossible just decades ago."

"Dani's boyfriend, Peter, told Chief Lambert what I'd seen. The chief asked me to assist on certain aspects of the case," Nell said.

"Did you accept the offer?" Ida asked.

"I did. We decided we might as well give it a try and see if I can find a clue of some kind."

"Or at least, provide another point of view or some insight that might have been ignored by everyone else," Violet pointed out. "I think Nell not only sees things in a different way than most of us, but she thinks about them or considers them from a very unique perspective."

"You might think about keeping some notes when you see the colors on people," John said. "It will probably take time to analyze what it all means, like if you see red coming from someone does it always mean the person is in danger? Could it mean the person is simply angry? Could it mean something entirely different? Keeping notes about the colors will help you understand the meanings they have."

Iris got up from her spot on the deck, walked

over to sit next to John, and rested her head on his knee.

"I think Iris likes the idea," Nell said causing the others to chuckle at the dog's input. "I'll make some notes when we go home tonight."

"It will help you organize what you're seeing so you'll be able to make sense of it," Violet said.

A sound like distant thunder rumbled in the distance and Nell's breath caught in her throat.

John noticed her distress, and understanding how the tornado she'd lived through caused Nell to react to storms, he attempted to comfort the young woman. "We aren't supposed to get any bad weather tonight. If it *was* thunder, it is miles and miles away from here. It could have been the rumble of a plane or the sound of something else."

Iris hurried over and Nell began to stroke the dog's head.

"Take some calming, deep breaths," Ida suggested in gentle voice. "That storm you experienced was very, very unusual for Massachusetts. The chances of another storm like that one is one in a trillion. You'll never be in another storm like that. You're safe."

Nell took in deep breaths and focused on what Ida had just said. She closed her eyes for a few moments paying attention to the warm breeze, the rustling of the leaves in the trees, and Iris's smooth fur under her hand. The feelings of panic slowly disappeared, and she lifted her lids. "I feel better."

Violet leaned over and hugged her sister. "I'm so glad."

Ida brought out a chocolate layer cake and a bowl of cut-up fruit and John passed around dessert plates.

"When will Bobby start work on your deck?" Ida asked once everyone had been served slices of the cake.

"He's going to come by tomorrow afternoon," Nell said, and suddenly she thought of the contract she and her sister had signed, and then recalled standing at the rental car company's counter talking to the employee who had waited on the man who leased the vehicle that had hit Pepper Forrest.

I should ask the police if I can see the rental car contract they took into evidence.

And then she wondered why the idea to look at the contract came into her mind.

14

Nell and Violet arrived on the Fuller University campus and found the small amphitheater where the memorial service would be held for Dr. Pepper Forrest. A reception room with drinks and light refreshments had been set up in a large conference space where about a hundred people had already congregated.

"Do you feel like we're crashing a party?" Violet leaned towards her sister.

"Sort of," Nell admitted, "but I'm guessing there are probably a good number of people here from the university who barely knew Pepper, but want to pay their respects."

"If anyone asks, we're going to say we met Pepper

in Bluewater and wanted to come down to acknowledge her at the service, right?" Violet asked.

"That's right. It's the truth, only we're leaving out the part about being involved in investigating the case."

Violet gave her sister an impish look as they approached the refreshment tables. "People don't need to know every detail."

They carried glasses of sparkling water and two small plates of hors d'oeuvres to a high table at the same time a young woman walked over from the opposite side.

"Mind sharing the table?" the dark-haired woman asked. "It's getting crowded in here."

"We're glad to," Violet said.

"I'm Julia," the woman said as she placed her glass of orange juice on the tabletop. Slim and stylish, she added, "I'm an administrative assistant in the chemistry department."

"This is my sister, Violet, and I'm Ellen, although everyone calls me Nell."

"Nice to meet you both," Julia told them. "Do you work here at the university?"

Violet explained how they'd briefly met Dr. Forrest in Bluewater when the professor had been visiting the town to attend a symposium and liked her instantly. "We wanted to come down to pay our respects."

"That's very nice of you," Julia said. "Pepper was a great person. I enjoyed talking with her. She was always helpful and easy-going."

"Did you know Pepper well?" Nell asked.

Julia said, "Well enough. We weren't best friends or anything, but we did go out a couple of times a month for drinks or dinner. We ran together three days a week. I really can't believe what's happened. I think I'm still in shock over it."

"Pepper told us she had lived in California for many years," Nell said. "I forgot which state she said she was born in." Nell hadn't forgotten, but she wanted to judge how much Pepper might have shared about her life with the young woman.

"She was born in New Hampshire. She and her parents moved to California when she was about eight-years old."

"What made her move to Boston?" Violet questioned.

"Pepper did her doctorate in at MIT and then stayed when she got a job offer," Julia said.

"She told us she'd been married, but that her husband died shortly after they were wed." Nell hoped to learn more information from Julia.

"What a sad story. Pepper and her boyfriend, his name was Justin, had been involved in an accident right after they got engaged. It took them months to heal and recover. Justin was in a second car accident about six or seven months after he and Pepper got married. He was killed."

"Was he alone in the car?" Violet asked.

"He was. It seems he lost control of the vehicle when he was driving on the coast road. Do you know what those roads are like?" Julia asked. "They wind like a snake and run right along the edge of the cliffs. He went off the road and crashed down the huge drop." The young woman visibly shuddered. "So terrible. I still cringe every time I think of it."

The sisters agreed with Julia that it was a terrible accident.

"Did Pepper move away right after the loss of her husband?" Nell asked.

"I think it was pretty soon after. I'm not exactly sure of the timeframe."

"Did you see Pepper pretty much every work-day?" Violet questioned.

"Yeah. Mondays through Fridays. It's so weird now. Sometimes I think I hear her coming into the department, and then I realize she's gone." Julia brushed at her eyes. "It's ironic, isn't it? Pepper and

Justin were in a bad crash during the time they were engaged, Justin died in an accident right after they got married, and then Pepper was killed in a hit-and-run car accident. Fate had it in for them, didn't it?"

Nell was pretty sure fate wasn't the reason for Pepper's death. "Did Pepper seem worried about anything lately?"

Julia straightened and blinked at Nell. "Why do you ask that?"

"Pepper seemed a little nervous when I talked to her," Violet said. "I'm not sure if nervous is the right word, maybe distracted would be a better description. She said she came to Bluewater on the spur of the moment. I didn't get the impression she was enjoying herself very much. I wondered if she and a boyfriend had broken up or maybe there might be something else going on."

"She wasn't seeing anyone at the moment," Julia said stiffly, but didn't address the question of whether or not Pepper had been worried or concerned about anything.

"What about work?" Nell asked. "Was she having trouble with anything here at the university?"

"I don't know anything about that." Julia swallowed the last of her beverage. "I'm going to go get a seat in the amphitheater. Nice to meet you." The young woman walked swiftly away.

"I think we touched a nerve," Violet said.

"I think you're right. But what was the cause? Julia seemed to think Pepper was worried about something, but what was it? And did it make her run away to Bluewater?"

A woman's voice said Nell's name from behind the sisters and when they turned, Nell saw Pepper's friend, Dr. Janis Littleton, walking towards them.

Nell introduced Violet to the woman, and then told her sister, "Dr. Littleton came to Bluewater shortly after Pepper's passing. I met her at The Sandy Rose Inn." Nell addressed her question to Dr. Littleton. "You spoke with the police after we met? Did they give you any answers?"

"I'm afraid it was a useless trip to talk to them," Janis said. "They wouldn't say much of anything. They told me they couldn't share much because it was an active investigation, but I also think it was because I was only a friend, not a relative." The professor let out a sigh. "You came down for the service?"

"We wanted to pay our respects, especially since we were some of the last people to see Pepper alive," Violet said.

Janis winced slightly at Violet's words. "I have not come to terms with the idea Pepper is gone and I won't ever see her again." The woman looked off across the room full of people. "You know, I've been thinking and thinking about it. Is it possible someone deliberately hit Pepper?"

"Who would do such a thing?" Nell asked, hoping that Janis had an idea about who might have been driving the car.

"Something's been bothering me," Janis said. "There was an incident about six months ago with a student of Pepper's. He was very angry about the grade he received. He was a senior. He blamed the bad grade for not getting the job he wanted. He told Pepper she'd ruined his life. The student complained to the dean over and over, but Pepper had the paperwork to back up the grade she'd assigned to him. He started to stalk her, even showing up outside her townhouse a few times. She was freaked out about it. When he graduated in December, the stalking stopped. I wonder if it started up again. I wonder if he followed Pepper to Bluewater and chased her down with his car."

Flutters of nervousness moved over Nell's skin. "Do you know the student's name?"

"David Belk."

"Is he still living in the Boston area?"

"He's a real estate agent in the city," Janis said. "I saw his photo online in a real estate advertisement."

"Do you know where he works?" Violet asked. "Do you remember the name of the firm?"

"CityPlace Realty." Janis looked like she might break down in tears. "Do you think that student hurt Pepper? Do you think he carried his grudge against her for the past six months?"

Nell wasn't sure about the young man and if he might have held onto his anger at Pepper after graduation, but she tried to calm the professor's fears. "I doubt it. He must have moved on, got the job, and forgot all about his college troubles."

"I hope so." Janis took in a long breath. "I hope he didn't have anything to do with Pepper's death." Passing a hand over her eyes, she said with a tentative tone, "Pepper told me something interesting. She said that right after her husband died in that accident on the California coast, she received a message from someone."

Nell's eyes widened. "What sort of a message?"

"Pepper told me it was threatening," Janis said. "I asked what was in the message, but she wouldn't say. She told me it had upset her. It was the main reason she left California."

"How did she receive the message?" Nell asked.

"It was in her home mailbox. It hadn't been mailed. Someone placed it in her box."

"Did she report it to the police?" Violet questioned.

"I don't know. When I brought it up a few weeks later, she wouldn't talk about it," Janis said. "She seemed sorry she brought it up with me."

People began to move out of the reception room and towards the amphitheater for the service.

"It was nice to see you. I'm going to find a colleague. We're supposed to sit together." Janis shook hands with the sisters and hurried away.

Nell and Violet joined the throng leaving the room.

"Pepper got a threatening message, huh?" Violet asked. "It worried her enough that she left California and moved to the East Coast. She was running from someone."

"It could have been a nut who read about the death of her husband and decided it would be fun to mess with a widow," Nell suggested. "It's something to add to the collection of details we have on Pepper."

"Definitely."

Nell moved closer to Violet. "I have an interest in renting an apartment here in the city."

"Oh, do you?" Violet gave her sister a sly smile. "Did this desire begin when Janis was telling us about the creepy student who was stalking Pepper? The one who became a real estate agent in Boston?"

"Possibly." The corners of Nell's mouth turned up. "You know me all too well."

"Should we pay a visit to David Belk after the service?" Nell questioned. "Talk to him about you wanting to rent an apartment?"

"I think that's a great idea."

"Yeah. I come up with a lot of great ideas," Violet joked. "Hopefully, this guy isn't a murderer. Talking to a killer isn't exactly the way I want to spend my afternoon."

"Should I go without you?" Nell asked.

"Fat chance." Violet playfully poked her sister with her elbow. "I can't let you have all the fun."

15

N ell and Violet sat at the glass table in the real estate office across from David Belk. The high-end realty firm was located on Boylston Street in Boston and the place had brick accent walls, a fireplace, modern lighting, tall windows, and comfortable stylish furniture.

David Belk looked to be in his early twenties, had light blond hair, cool blue eyes, and was dressed in a slim-fitting gray suit.

"Tell me what you're looking for in an apartment." David clicked at his laptop.

"Well, I'd like one or two bedrooms, two bathrooms, a nice kitchen, preferably white. An outdoor space would be wonderful. I don't need parking. I'd also like the kitchen to be open to the living area."

"What part of the city would you prefer to be in?" David asked.

"Back Bay, or over in the Fenway. Maybe Beacon Hill." Nell was enjoying playing a wealthy young woman looking for a place to spend weekends.

"And what is your budget?"

Nell made up a figure and the real estate agent looked pleased about what she planned to spend on rent.

"I have several nice apartments I think you'd like." David adjusted his screen to show the sisters the available places.

"Those look great," Nell said as David paged through the online photos. "Those might be something I'd like."

Violet asked, "How did you get involved in real estate?"

"I graduated college last December and answered ads. I've always been interested in real estate. It's like being an entrepreneur or a business owner. It's the perfect career for me. I get to meet so many different people and I enjoy finding the right home for a client."

"Where did you graduate from?" Nell asked.

David told them the name of the Boston university.

"A very good school," Violet said. "Did you happen to know that professor who got killed recently on the North Shore? She taught at that college."

David seemed to stiffen and he sniffed. "I knew her."

"Did you?" Violet questioned. "Were you in one of her classes?"

"Yes, I was." David's upper lip tightened.

Nell asked the name of the class and David told her what it was.

"Did you enjoy the course?" Violet questioned. "It sounds really interesting."

"The course was fine. The instructor was not." David sat straight in his chair.

Violet leaned forward pretending everything she heard was new information to her. "What was wrong with the professor?"

"She was a terrible instructor. Her exams were ridiculous. She took issue with everything in the answers we wrote. She was very nit-picky. The grades she gave out did not reflect the knowledge her students had acquired and demonstrated."

"Did you complain to the university about Dr. Forrest?" Violet asked the young man.

"Of course, I did, and it was to no avail. They

wouldn't look into my complaints. They allowed my poor grade to stand. It kept me from receiving offers from several well-known firms. Pepper Forrest was a terrible instructor. Honestly? She ruined my career prospects. I would have liked to do the same to her." David's face had changed from professional and pleasant to angry and indignant.

"Were other students disgruntled about their grades?" Nell asked.

"Sure, but I didn't care about them. I cared about myself and how the poor grade would impact my job prospects," David said adjusting the pewter cufflink on his sleeve.

"Did you speak with Dr. Forrest about the grade she'd given to you?" Violet watched the young's man's expression.

"Yes, many times. She blew me off. Can you imagine? A professor so uncaring that she would blow off a student's questions and comments. She was unfit to teach," David said. "She should have been fired."

Nell could see the flush of anger on David's cheeks as his face hardened and he began to rant about Dr. Forrest's incompetence.

David said, "I'm not sure she was actually incompetent, but she was lazy and arrogant and didn't care what some lowly undergraduate student had to say. It made me feel used and powerless. She held all the cards. I was less than a pauper. I had no rights at all. I'm glad to be out of there and in a place where I can be judged on my merits."

"It sounds like you made the right choice in accepting an offer here." Nell thought the young real estate agent was getting overly excited about his past professor and wanted David to calm down before his emotions got the best of him.

"I could have done better." David steamed. "You know what? Dr. Forrest got exactly what she deserved."

"You really don't mean that," Violet suggested.

David stared at Violet with hate in his eyes.

"It was an unfortunate situation you had to deal with," Violet said. "But something positive may have come out of the difficulty. Perhaps it made you more resilient."

David's face was now the color of a beet. "What a bunch of hogwash. That's what losers say when something bad happens and they can't maneuver their way out of it." He added in a sickeningly sweet and mocking tone of voice, "You must have been empowered by being treated like garbage. It must have made you stronger." He pounded the table with the palm of his hand. "It didn't. Get it through your head. Nothing positive came out of it."

Nell's blood began to boil. "How dare you speak to my sister like that. We came in here looking for an apartment, not a fight. We simply brought up someone we knew who worked at the university, but you decided to have a rant."

David stood up and leaned menacingly across his desk.

Nell stood and stared directly into the man's eyes. "We're done here."

Violet followed her sister's lead.

"You come in here and waste my time," David raised his voice.

"You wasted *our* time by obsessing over someone who has nothing to do with you or your life anymore," Nell explained evenly. She did not like David's behavior one bit, and she felt intimidated by his negativity and his bizarre outburst.

Suddenly, David's body and clothes were covered in a deep shade of green. The color shimmered over him for several seconds, and then turned to black.

Nell took several quick steps back while she watched the colors change from black to green. Reaching for her sister's arm, she tugged on it. "It's time to go," she told Violet and they backed out of the office.

"I'll thank you not to waste my time ever again." David gave them a menacing look.

Nell slammed the door to the man's office and she and Violet stormed away.

Sipping coffees a few blocks away, the sisters sat shaken by the interaction with David Belk.

"That guy is certified looney." Violet rubbed her neck. "We only asked an innocent question about a former professor and he went off the deep end. That nutty obsession with her and his poor grade. He graduated. It's over. He can't let it go. He could easily be the one who drove that car into Pepper."

Nell took a deep breath. "I saw colors on him."

Violet looked at her sister. "What colors?"

"Green and black." Nell felt slightly woozy from the meeting with the real estate agent.

"What do those colors mean? What do they stand for?" Violet's voice sounded a little bit shaky.

"Remember colors don't mean the same things in every society? They have different meanings in different cultures."

"Like what? Tell me some of them," Violet said.

Nell read from the notes she'd made on her phone. "Black can mean mystery, and death."

Violet's shoulders moved back and she groaned. "Does it ever stand for something else?"

"It can also stand for life, and resurrection."

"Two completely different things." Violet pushed a strand of hair from her eye. "I'm going to go out on a limb here and guess the black color doesn't represent life in this case. It's more apt to mean death. I hate to ask, but what does a green color mean?"

"Green can stand for wisdom or rebirth," Nell said reading from her phone. "It can mean envy, too."

"I think the green on David Belk would indicate envy," Violet said. "I hope Chief Lambert or another officer from Bluewater has questioned David. You'd better ask him. This is a guy that law enforcement needs to be aware of." Violet lowered her voice. "Can't you picture David committing a crime? He seems full of himself and he seems to lack empathy. I wonder where he was on the afternoon of Pepper's accident."

"David frightened me," Nell admitted.

"He frightened me, too. He shouldn't be working with the public if he can't control his emotions."

"He was so helpful and nice when we first got there, and after we asked him about Pepper, he completely transformed. It was like he couldn't stop himself," Nell said.

Nell frowned. "Not being able to control yourself isn't a very good characteristic to have. Depending on the severity of the issue, losing control could lead someone to commit a crime."

Violet eyed her sister. "You mean like murder?"

16

Nell, Violet, and Dani were dividing the check for their dinner at a town pub when Nell noticed Rob and the new researcher, Atkins Murray, standing at the crowded bar. Rob waved and gestured for them to join him and Atkins.

"Why is Rob with Atkins?" Dani asked with a sniff. "What if that guy is Pepper's killer?"

"Let's go find out why they're out together," Nell suggested.

The young women went over to the bar to greet the men, and Atkins was introduced to Dani and Violet.

Once conversation started up, Nell leaned close

to Rob. "Why are you out with Atkins? Aren't you suspicious of him?"

Rob said, "I *am* suspicious, but we don't have any facts or details to link him to Pepper's accident. Atkins asked me if I'd like to go out for a couple of beers. I agreed in order to get to know him better. Talking to him more will either confirm he's Pepper's attacker or it will make our working relationship better ... so here I am. It's win-win."

"I guess so." Nell didn't like the idea that Rob was socializing with a potential criminal. "Have you learned anything from him?"

"We've haven't even been here for fifteen minutes," Rob said. "We've barely found a place to stand, it's so crowded in here. We just ordered beers. I haven't had a chance yet to ask Atkins if he's Pepper's killer."

"Ha ha," Nell deadpanned.

Atkins looked over at Rob from his discussion with Violet and Dani. "Did you say my name?"

"What?" Rob stammered, attempting to keep his tone even and innocent. "No, I didn't. You must have misheard."

Atkins returned to his conversation with the two young women.

"Don't ask me anything more about him when he's standing only a few yards away," Rob whispered.

"Oh, don't be so fussy," Nell said. "He can't hear what we're saying to each other."

Rob gave Nell a look that told her he didn't think much of her comment.

Just then Peter and Detective Michael Gregory walked over, and as Peter leaned down to give Dani a kiss, the detective introduced himself to those he didn't know and gave Nell an especially warm greeting.

"I hear you and Peter went on an outing together?" Gregory asked Nell.

"Did we?" Nell knew the detective was referring to her and Peter's visit to the rental car agency. "I seem to have forgotten."

"Did you find out anything helpful when you were there?" Gregory asked.

"I'm not sure I know what you mean." Nell pretended to be confused about what Gregory was alluding to.

Detective Gregory chuckled. "You don't need to be so wary around me. I don't bite, and anyway, we're on the same team."

Nell gave Peter a quick a look and said to the detective, "I'm not on a team."

"I know you're working with the police, Nell," the detective told her. "I know it's some informal thing and I'm not going to ask you questions about your involvement, but we need to help each other so this thing can get solved." A sincere smile crossed the man's lips.

"Okay, Detective," Nell said feeling warmth creep up her neck. "I wish I had discovered some earth-shattering news, but I didn't. Otherwise, I'd share with you."

"Call me, Michael."

"Michael." Nell's cheeks felt like they were on fire and she wished the detective didn't have such an effect on her. "Do you have anything to share?"

"Not really." The detective reached for the bottle of beer the bartender was handing to him. "It's like the driver of that car has vanished into thin air and isn't coming back."

"No leads?" Nell asked, as she accepted a drink from her sister.

"Plenty of leads." Michael Gregory leaned against the bar. "They're all good for nothing though."

Nell thought for a few seconds. "If the killer lived in Bluewater, he could have been back at home in a very short amount of time. He probably parked his own car near the mall, ditched the rental car there after he hit and killed Pepper, then got into his own vehicle and calmly drove home."

"Yeah. Sort of like looking for a needle in a haystack," Michael said. "No prints were found in the rental car. There was nothing at the rental company except a video of the man renting the car wearing a disguise ... so no clues there either. The guy wore a disguise when he was driving the car so witnesses couldn't get a good look at him. The fake ID used to rent the vehicle led nowhere. Unless we get a tip or find something new, I'm afraid the death will go unexplained and the person responsible will go unpunished."

"Are you always this cheery?" Nell joked with the detective to lighten the mood.

"Always," Michael kidded. "My colleagues call me Cheerful Mike."

Nell laughed. "So what do you do in situations like this? Seriously."

"We hope, we might say a prayer, we keep looking until a tiny thing leads to a bigger thing." Michael took a swallow from his beer bottle.

Nell told the detective about her and Violet's trip to Boston earlier in the day. "Has anyone talked to you or the local police about a former student of

Pepper's? His name is David Belk. He put up a stink when Pepper gave him a bad grade. He stalked her for a while."

Michael stood straighter. "Who told you this?"

"Professor Janis Littleton. She was a friend of Pepper's."

Michael nodded. "I read the notes about her visit to the station. She didn't mention anything about the student stalking Pepper."

"She told us she'd been thinking things over and over and David Belk worried her."

"A university administrator told us about the student and his behavior. Some officers had a talk with Mr. Belk. He claimed his disappointment in his grade was overblown and he'd never stalked Dr. Forrest. He acted indignant about it."

"Did Belk lose his temper when the officers spoke with him?" Nell asked.

"There wasn't any mention of that," Michael said.

Nell reported how Belk had behaved with her and her sister when they met with him. "When we brought up Dr. Forrest, he changed into a fire-breathing dragon. His loss of emotional control was a little frightening."

"And why did you and your sister go to talk to him?" Michael asked.

Nell looked at the detective with a sideways glance. "We were interested in renting an apartment in the city."

"Why?"

"It would be nice to spend some time there," Nell said.

"You aren't planning a move to Boston?"

"No, Bluewater is our home, but we thought it might be nice to have a place to stay in the city."

"And you just happened to be at the real estate agency where David Belk works?" Michael gave Nell a disbelieving expression.

Nell sighed and admitted, "We looked him up. We didn't think it would hurt to talk to him."

"It *didn't* hurt for you to talk to him. In fact, it was helpful. His behavior warrants another visit from us."

"Did Belk *not* lose his temper when the officers talked with him about Pepper because they were law enforcement?" Nell questioned. "Was Belk being more careful not to reveal his true feelings because he was talking to the police, but with Violet and me there was no reason to rein in his emotions so he let loose?"

"That's probably right. He did a good job hiding his feelings in front of law enforcement when they went to talk to him."

"We also heard about an accident Pepper and her fiancé had been in," Nell said.

"Yeah. Months before their wedding, they were involved in an accident. They were badly injured and there was a fatality."

"A fatality?" Nell nearly shuddered.

"A woman was killed. She was in the other car," Michael said with a nod.

Before Nell could ask anything more, Rob interrupted the discussion between Nell and the detective. "How about you two join in with the rest of us. What's all the whispering about?"

"We're not whispering." Michael smiled and turned around to the others. "If we were, we wouldn't have been able to hear one another with the music and all the chatter in here."

The group stood together talking for about ten minutes before they split again into conversations of two or three. Nell, Rob, and Atkins discussed the research the men were conducting at the hospital and Nell hoped Rob wouldn't bring up doing an evaluation on her ability to see emotions in front of Atkins.

When Rob stepped to the bar to order some drinks, Nell and Atkins stood awkwardly with one another.

Nell said, "The police still haven't found the driver of the car that hit Pepper Forrest."

Atkins eyes clouded over. "That's unfortunate."

"I can't stop thinking about the day. My sister and I were standing near the window. I saw that car tearing away from the curb and heading right for her." Nell's shoulders trembled. "Were you at the lab when you heard about the accident?"

"I heard about it at home when I watched the news," Atkins said.

"Had you been in the lab that day?" Nell worked at getting Atkins to tell her where he was when the accident had happened.

"I don't remember the day. I'm usually in the lab in the mornings."

"What do you do after the lab? Do you usually go back to your office?"

"Much of the time, I do. On occasion, there's a guest lecturer visiting the hospital and I go to hear the speaker. Or I do rounds in the hospital as a consultant to some of the physicians. Other times, I write."

"You don't remember where you were when the

accident happened?" Nell asked one more time with a gentle tone of voice.

Atkins's jaw was set as he looked into Nell's eyes. "I already answered that question."

Nell watched as Atkin's slowly washed over with red from the top of his head all the way down to his shoes.

He abruptly moved away from her and started a conversation with Peter leaving Nell blinking at the spot where the researcher had been standing.

17

Iris rested in a patch of shade next to where Nell, wearing a baseball cap to keep the sun out of her eyes, worked at her easel set up right off of the cliff walk pathway. People strolling by stopped to admire the seascape painting that was receiving its finishing touches.

The picture wasn't an ordinary painting of sea and sky, cliffs, sand, and waves. It burst with every paint color that was humanly possible to create, which was inadequate and impossible to match what Nell saw in nature.

Some people who stopped asked questions and she was always happy to answer especially if it was a young person or a child who showed interest in artwork.

The day was pleasantly warm and clear and she and Violet had plans to meet later for a quick swim in the ocean.

"Hey, look who's here."

Nell recognized the man's voice and looked up to see Detective Michael Gregory heading towards her.

Iris bounced over to greet the man and she was rewarded with some pats on her head and neck.

The detective stood slightly behind Nell's stool so he could get a good look at what she was painting. "Whoa. What style is this? It is impressionist?"

"Sort of," Nell smiled. "Some people might call it that."

"There's so much color to it. It's stunning," the detective told her.

"I've always seen a lot of colors in the world," Nell said.

"Well, no one sees all the colors you have in this painting. When I look out at the sea and the sky, I see blue. I also see white sand."

"What else do you see?" Nell asked. "Look again. Pay more attention."

Michael looked around the cliffs and down at the waves crashing onto the beach. "Green in the grass, reddish-pink flowers, white foam on the waves as they hit the beach."

"Does the foam sparkle or is it flat white?"

"It sparkles. It's kind of glittery."

"What about the grass?" Nell asked. "Is it all just green?"

Michael moved his gaze around the pathway and over the cliffs. "No. There are different shades of green, a little bit of it is almost yellow."

"So it seems you're seeing far more colors than you first told me you saw."

"I guess so." Michael grinned at Nell. "But nowhere near what's on that canvas of yours."

"If you train yourself, you'll be able to see more," Nell said. "If you really look deeply at things, you'll surprise yourself with what you can see."

"I'm not sure about that. I don't have an artist's eye."

"Everyone has an artist's eye," Nell said. "But not everyone sees what they're capable of."

"This is beginning to sound like a philosophy class," Michael said.

"And you thought you were just out for a walk." Nell pulled the brim of the baseball cap down a little to keep the sun from shining directly into her eyes.

"This is a beautiful town. I don't know how I haven't been here before this."

"It's easy to miss," Nell said. "Bluewater doesn't

get the same attention that Salem or Gloucester or Newburyport get. We're kind of tucked away. A lot of people have never heard about the great beaches here or about the good shopping and dining. I think that's starting to change. Violet and I notice more people here in the summers and more people coming earlier in the season."

"It will mean more business for your shop," Michael said.

Nell laughed. "We don't want to be too busy. Violet and I want to enjoy the summer, too."

Michael's face turned serious. "Chief Lambert and I are going to Boston in a few days to speak with David Belk."

"Good." Nell was relieved that the officers would pay Belk another visit and would be able to use their experience to assess the young man.

"The chief didn't tell me why he asked you to help out on the case," Michael said. "Did you work in law enforcement in the past?"

Nell looked up at the man, but didn't say anything right away. "What *did* Chief Lambert say?"

"He told me he knew your parents. He said they'd passed away. The chief said he knew you and Violet from when your family spent summers here. He said you and your sister were very perceptive and that you would be a new and different set of eyes on the case."

"That about sums it up." Nell gave a nod.

A grin worked at the edges of Michael's lips. "You aren't going to tell me about your special skills and experience?"

"Nope."

"Okay, I won't ask about it again." Michael shrugged. "Maybe that's a lie. I might ask about it again."

"You can ask all you like," Nell told him with a sparkle in her eye. "But if I were you, I wouldn't waste the time."

NELL AND VIOLET spent almost an hour swimming and riding the waves on their boogie boards. The dog jumped and ran and raced the waves under the perfect blue sky until she needed a rest and joined the two women on the beach blanket sunning themselves.

"That was the best. The water isn't even that cold," Nell told her sister as they warmed up in the sun.

Violet gave Nell a look like she was crazy. "The

water was like ice. I don't know how we stayed in for so long."

"Because it was fun, that's why. And like Dad always said, we're both part fish."

They rubbed at their limbs with the beach towels to get the circulation going again.

Nell had told Violet that Detective Gregory had run into her while she'd been working on a painting on the cliff walk.

"He's cute, isn't he?" Violet teased her sister.

"He's an attractive man, yes. He also seems very nice."

"Did he ask you out yet?"

"No, he didn't." Nell gave Violet a playful poke.

"You need to act more interested," Violet suggested.

"No, I don't. I don't want to get involved with anyone. Anyway, he'll be gone when this case is solved, so what would be the point of starting something?"

"Maybe he'll stay in Bluewater," Violet said.

"Most likely, he won't." Nell put on her sunglasses and her baseball hat. "He and Chief Lambert are going to speak with David Belk."

"Oh, good," Violet said with a sense of relief. "They can figure out if Belk is dangerous or not."

"They'll look into where Belk was at the time of the accident. That could easily eliminate him as a suspect."

"And what about Atkins Murray?" Violet slipped a t-shirt over her swimsuit. "You saw the red on him again when we were all at the pub. He seemed to play dumb about his whereabouts for the timeframe when Pepper was hit by the car. I'm going to bet he remembers very well where he was. Did you tell Chief Lambert that you saw red on Atkins?"

"I told him. He's going to look into where Atkins was on that day."

Violet used the towel to dry her long, straight hair. "Did you ask the chief if you could get a look at the car rental agreement the killer signed when he leased the car he used to hit Pepper?"

"I'm going to the police station the day after tomorrow to see it," Nell said.

"What do you expect to see when you look at it?"

"I don't have any idea. I just got the idea that I should look at it, see how the killer signed it. I don't know. Maybe it will lead to a clue. Or not." Nell frowned. "Most likely, it will be a dead end."

"The chief also has three witnesses lined up for you to speak with," Violet pointed out.

"Would you come with me when I meet with them? I'm feeling nervous about it."

"Of course, I'll come. Beforehand, we can go over the questions we should ask them about the day," Violet suggested.

"This is such a mess," Nell sighed. "How can a killer commit a crime and slip away so easily? What if he's never found?"

"He'll be found. It might take a while, but he'll be found eventually."

"Why did Pepper come to Bluewater out of the blue?" Nell tried to examine the details they knew. "She came on her own without inviting her colleague and friend to the symposium."

"Coming here wasn't a big trip for her. She lived only about thirty minutes away. It seems that Pepper needed a break, she wanted to go to the symposium, maybe she needed to recharge. She also wanted to speak with a private detective so she needed to get away alone."

"She made an appointment with a PI," Nell pointed out. "I think she needed alone time, but not because she needed rest. She needed to quietly meet with a private investigator." Nell turned a little on the blanket so she could better see her sister. "What was going on in her life? She thought someone was following her?"

"That, yes, and because we think she was trying to locate someone," Violet said. "But who was it?"

"It's also interesting that Pepper didn't drive herself here," Nell said.

"Why?"

"I don't think she wanted to bring her own car because if someone was following her, he'd most likely know the make and model of the car," Nell said. "She could be less conspicuous if she hired a car service to take her here, and then used the trolley service when she was in town. She could hide among the tourists."

"Who in the world was she hiding from?" Violet asked. "Why was she hiding? What was the reason? Who was after her? Who wanted her dead?"

The million dollar questions, Nell thought. *How is the killer ever going to be found?*

18

After the workday had finished, Nell and Violet decided to take a bike ride on the state park trails. On the way out to the garage to get the bikes, they heard the sound of a hammer and then a man cursing.

"Bobby's working on the deck." Violet rolled her eyes. "He's been kind of sullen the past few times he's been here. He acts angry and impatient and curses every few minutes. I asked him a question the other day and he acted really annoyed about it. He was pleasant when he was here to give us the estimate, but I guess that goes out the window once he actually gets the job."

"John and Ida warned us Bobby had mood swings. It seems they were right."

The garage bays were located to the left of the deck and the sisters had to pass by it to get the bikes from inside.

Nell called a greeting to the man who didn't even bother to look up. Because his dismissive manner annoyed Nell, she walked over to where Bobby was preparing to lay a board. "How's the work going?"

Bobby glanced at her with a frown. "It's going."

"We're heading out for a while. Need anything before we go?"

"I'm good." Bobby picked up his nail gun and started to place the nails.

When Nell went into the garage for her bicycle, Violet had already checked the tires. "I guess he's not so much for small talk, huh?"

"So it seems."

Nell looked up to see Bobby standing in front of the garage bay.

"Sorry," he said. "I don't mean to be rude. I've got a lot on my mind. I have some decisions to make and it's wearing me down. I wanted to apologize."

"It's okay," Nell told him. "No worries."

Bobby returned to the deck work and the sisters exchanged looks of surprise.

"I wasn't expecting that," Violet said. "It was nice of him to apologize."

The sisters rode down Main Street and took a left on a country road that led to the entrance to the state park. The paths were dappled with the sunlight filtering through the tall trees as Nell and Violet made their way to one of the more challenging trails in the park. The view from the top was so striking that the young women thought the difficult ride was worth the effort.

Nell puffed as they made their way up one of the steep hills. "I'm rethinking whether or not reaching the top is worth this pain."

Violet laughed. "Just think about how easy the ride down will be."

Nell answered with a groan.

They were drenched with sweat by the time they reached the top and they drank greedily from their water bottles.

Nell removed her helmet, poured some water into her hand, and spilled it over her face and neck. "That was rough. I didn't think I was so out of shape."

"You're not out of shape. It's our first hard bike ride of the summer."

The sisters sat on a rock and admired the pretty view of the hills, the town, and the ocean stretching far out to the horizon. White, puffy clouds floated slowly against the deep blue of the sky.

"You're going to the police station tomorrow to look at the rental agreement?" Violet asked.

"I'm meeting the chief at 6pm. Early in the morning, I'm meeting with the three witnesses. Can you still come with me to that? I don't know why, but I'm feeling nervous about the whole day. And I'll have so little time to spend on any of my commission work."

"Don't worry. You'll get it all done on time. You're almost finished with the paintings you're doing for William." The innkeeper at The Sandy Rose commissioned Nell to paint three small seascapes each with a different boat in the picture.

"Yeah." Nell took a swallow from her water bottle. "I'm feeling rushed. I'm also feeling useless helping on this case."

"You've reported several important details. You've told the chief about Atkins and how he seemed very annoyed when you asked him where he was when Pepper was killed, you reported on David Belk's behavior when we met with him, you told them Pepper had made an appointment with a private investigator. Those were things they didn't know."

Nell blew out a long breath. "You're right, but it just doesn't seem like enough. I'm glad I'm an artist and a graphic designer because I'm not cut out to work full time for the police. It's so difficult to find the answers that can solve crimes. I'd be frustrated all the time. I'd always feel like I was letting people down."

"I think I'd feel the same way," Violet admitted. "Thank heavens there are people who can handle the job."

"I've been thinking about Pepper a lot," Nell said. "She didn't have it easy, did she? Her parents died young, she didn't have any other relatives. Then there was the car accident she was in with her fiancé where they both suffered serious injuries."

"And then her new husband died in a crash several months after they were married." Violet shook her head.

"Pepper was afraid of something. She was worried enough about it that she was planning to see a private detective," Nell said. "She died before she could make it to the appointment. Do you think her worry and her death are connected or is it a terrible coincidence that she was killed when she was visiting Bluewater?"

Violet thought it over while she redid her braid. "I'm leaning towards the two things being connected."

Nell asked, "Was Pepper her real name or was that a nickname?"

"Most everything on the news refers to her as Pepper," Violet said, "but didn't one article mention that was her nickname? What was her real name? Let me think. Priscilla? Penelope? Patricia? I can't remember, but I'd bet money I read or heard that Pepper was just a nickname." Violet faced her sister. "Why does it matter?"

"I don't know. I feel like it does somehow."

"You can look it up when you get home."

"Her friends told us Pepper didn't like to do things alone," Nell said. "They were surprised she came to Bluewater by herself to attend the symposium. And they said it seemed like a spur of the moment decision." With a soft voice, she added, "Pepper must have been afraid of something and she must have known it was getting closer to her. That's why I was able to see her feelings of worry, her feelings that danger was nipping at her heels. Her emotions were so strong that they manifested visually."

"It makes perfect sense," Violet nodded.

"Why did someone want her dead?" Nell asked. "If we can figure that out, I think the *why* will probably lead us to the *who*."

IT WAS LATE, but Nell was still sitting at her workstation in the studio, with Iris sleeping at her feet, trying to make headway on all the design work she had to get done. She glanced out the window and as the menacing darkness sent a shiver of unease through her body, she was comforted by the streetlamps shining golden spots of light here and there on the sidewalk outside ... little pools of hope in a dangerous world.

Sitting in front of her computer monitor, she tapped a pencil absent-mindedly against the desktop considering the logo and website design she was working on for a local accounting firm, and then she remembered she wanted to look up Pepper's real name.

Tapping at her keyboard, she brought up articles reporting the hit-and-run incident and read through them trying to find mention of the woman's birth name, but couldn't find anything about it. Wading through the many stories, she finally gave up thinking it must have been a television news report where she heard Pepper's real name.

The police must have her given name, Nell realized and decided to ask about it when she was at the station in the morning.

Looking at the time, Nell yawned. "Come on, Iris. Let's call it a day and go to bed."

Iris got up and did a long, slow stretch as Nell was about to shut down her computer. She stopped when the idea came into her head that the university website might have Pepper's biography posted online.

Bringing up the chemistry department site, she scrolled through the professors and staff section until she found the entry about Pepper.

Penelope "Pepper" Forrest was born in New Hampshire and moved with her parents to California when she was a young child. Graduating from college with honors, she worked for several years as a high school teacher before moving to the Boston area to study for her Ph.D.

Penelope.

Nell stared at the photograph of Pepper smiling out at her from the corner of the biography and her heart contracted.

What happened to you? Who wanted you dead? How did you know someone was after you? You were only thirty-four. There was so much life left to live. How long had this person been chasing you down? How long had you been afraid for your life?

Anger flooded Nell's veins as she stared into the woman's eyes ... and then she made a vow and spoke it aloud.

"We'll figure it out. I'll help the police find the person responsible for taking your life. I won't give up. I promise."

19

The Bluewater Public Library was a stone, two-story building with black shutters at the windows set on a landscaped acre of trees, flowering bushes, pachysandra, and flowers planted in the borders around the periphery of the property.

Nell and Violet met the three accident witnesses in the small, back conference room with rich wood-paneled walls, gleaming hardwood floors, and large windows that let in the light and looked over the pretty property.

Happy to be in the library instead of the bare, utilitarian police station, Nell was able to relax in the informal setting as she and Violet took seats at the polished table to await the arrival of the witnesses.

Three people came into the room within five minutes of one another. All were residents of Bluewater. There were other witnesses besides the three Nell and Violet were meeting with who were on the street when Pepper had been hit, but they did not see the accident itself.

Shelby Porter was a thirty-one-year-old nurse practitioner who had been shopping for her young daughter's birthday gift before hurrying off to see a client.

Mick Jones, twenty-four, a tall, slim musician who played in an area band, had his hair cut longer on one side and wore a small, gold, hoop nose ring.

Marjorie Wallis was a sixty-three-year-old math teacher at the town middle school who had been running errands before heading to her spin class.

When everyone had settled around the table and introduced themselves, Nell thanked them all for meeting. "My sister and I were in our shop standing by the front door and the windows. I heard and saw the car racing down the road. I didn't see it hit the woman." She swallowed. "But I heard the impact."

Marjorie Wallis closed her eyes for a few seconds and took in a long breath.

Nell asked if they could talk about what they'd

been doing in town and what they saw of the accident.

Marjorie said, "After I left school, I did a few errands on Main Street. I bought a gift card at one of the restaurants for an anniversary gift for a couple of our friends. I also ran into the sporting goods store to get some athletic socks and I stopped at the candy store to get some candy for my husband. I had just stepped outside onto the sidewalk when the accident happened."

Shelby explained that she'd run into the children's store to pick up a couple of presents for her daughter's upcoming birthday. "I was walking to my car when the man hit that woman. It happened right in front of me. I'll never forget it. It all seemed to happen in slow motion."

Marjorie nodded in agreement. "It plays in my head over and over. I wish I could have yelled to the woman to alert her, but it all happened too fast."

Mick Jones said, "I was in the music shop. I picked up some new strings for my guitar. We had a gig that night in Boston. I stepped outside and was waiting to cross the street further up from the woman who got hit. That car shot down the street like a rocket. I was about to step into the road, but held up when I heard the roar of the engine as the guy accelerated away from the curb." He shook his head in disgust. "Idiot."

"And you all saw the impact?" Nell asked.

The three people nodded.

"I'm not going to ask you to describe what you saw when the car hit Dr. Forrest."

The three faces looked relieved to hear that.

Nell asked, "If you could, would you be able to tell us what happened right before Dr. Forrest was hit? Did she see the oncoming car? And would you speak about anything you noticed about the car and the driver?"

Mick went first. "Like I said, I could have been hit by the jerk, but I heard him coming and was able to keep from stepping any further into the street."

"Think back on the experience," Nell suggested. "Had you taken steps into the road before you stopped yourself from advancing any further?"

"Yeah, I took, maybe, two steps into Main Street and then stopped."

"Did the driver see you in the road?"

Mick thought back on the day. "You know ... I think he did see me. He swerved a little."

"To avoid hitting you?" Nell asked.

"Yeah, maybe," Mick said. "He wasn't that close to me. I think he saw me about to cross. I think I remember him swerving the car a little towards the middle of the road in case I got further into the street."

"Did he swerve when he saw Dr. Forrest?"

Mick looked down at the table for a few seconds, and before lifting his head, he said, "No. The guy accelerated. He aimed right for her." The young musician shrugged. "That's what it looked and sounded like to me from my vantage point."

"Did the professor see the oncoming car?" Nell asked.

"At the last second, yeah," Mick said. "It was too late though."

Shelby said, "I was walking in the direction of my car. I'd parked at a meter on Main Street. I was in a hurry, thinking about all the things I had to do for my daughter's party. I was on the same side of the street where my car was parked so I didn't have to cross the street. I saw the car speeding down the road. He was going way too fast. I gave him a dirty look as he zoomed by me. I turned my head to watch him go past. That's when he hit the woman."

"Did he slow before he hit her?" Nell asked.

"No, he didn't." Shelby's jaw was set in disgust. "It seemed like he sped up."

"Do you think he saw her in the road?"

"He'd have to be blind not to have seen her."

"Could he have been on his phone or looking down at something inside his car and didn't see Dr. Forrest in the road?"

"I don't think so," Mick said. "He seemed to see me. It seemed like he tried to avoid me."

"He certainly didn't try to avoid the professor," Marjorie Wallis chimed in. "I'd just come out of the candy store. I was right on the sidewalk a few yards from Dr. Forrest. She stepped into the street. I heard the car's engine roar like the driver had gunned it. It looked intentional to me. He saw her in the road. He had no intention of stopping. It was like watching someone get murdered right before your eyes."

Nell silently agreed with Marjorie. It *was* murder, and it took place in broad daylight on the Main Street of a small town.

"Do you think this guy hit the woman on purpose?" Mick asked Nell.

Nell replied, "I didn't see the car after it went by our shop. I didn't see the approach it took ... whether it sped up or slowed down or tried to avoid hitting her."

"He did *not* try to avoid her." Marjorie's voice was adamant.

"I didn't see any indication that the driver tried to

avoid hitting the woman. As I said, he seemed to speed up." Shelby rubbed at the back of her shoulders. "But I don't know if I can say it was intentional. Maybe it was the result of distracted driving."

"I don't think the driver was distracted at all," Mick said. "He was facing forward, not looking down. He had to have seen Dr. Forrest."

"Can you describe what the man looked like?" Nell asked. "It was definitely a man? Could it have been a woman?"

Mick's eyes widened. "No. It was a guy. I'd put money on that. The shoulders, the way he held the wheel. It wasn't a woman."

"What do you mean about his shoulders?" Nell questioned.

"He had the shoulders of a guy, wider. Broader."

"What about his hair?"

"It was longer, kind of poorly cut," Mick said. "Being a musician, I pay attention to people's appearances. We have to look a certain way on stage. Hair, clothes, attitudes, it all plays into the performance. People can be the best musicians in the world, but if there isn't any performance quality and energy, then the crowd won't be impressed."

"Is there anything you remember about the driver's face?"

"Not really." Mick shook his head. "The car flew past. I noticed the hair because it was a little longer and messy-looking. The guy had on sunglasses, too, so the eyes were hidden from view. That's all I can tell you about him."

"I only saw the car from the side," Marjorie said. "I didn't notice anything about the driver. I *do* think he had a hat on." She looked to Mick for confirmation."

"Yeah," Mick said. "A hat. One of those winter kinds of hats. You know the kind some guys wear all year round? Fits over the head, but flops a little in the back."

Shelby sighed. "I didn't see the man in the car very well at all. When he came towards me, the sun was creating a glare on the windshield so I didn't get a good look at him. I couldn't say if he had on sunglasses or was wearing a hat. I wasn't paying much attention either. Sorry."

"Did the driver slow the car after hitting Dr. Forrest?" Nell asked.

"I don't remember," Shelby said. "I was so horrified by the accident that I was totally focused on the woman lying in the street. I just stood there for a few seconds, staring in disbelief. Then my medical training kicked in and I rushed to her to see if I could help her."

Nell watched Marjorie turn red before she said, "That driver didn't slow at all. He seemed to want to get out of there as fast as he could. He floored it. I didn't watch the car take off, but I distinctly heard the sound of the engine speeding up."

"That's right," Mick agreed. Red color completely shaded his body. "As soon as he hit her, he drove even faster. He didn't hesitate to see what happened to her. I don't care what the police think. I was there. I saw it. That guy hit the professor on purpose."

20

"An officer is getting the lease contract from evidence storage," Chief Lambert said. "We're going to Boston to interview David Belk a second time."

Nell sat at the table next to the chief in his cramped office. The big wooden desk was piled high with folders and notebooks and his desktop computer, and the table they sat at had a stack of colored folders and the man's laptop.

"Don't mind the mess," Chief Lambert said with a low chuckle. "I have my own personal filing methods. It works." The chief gestured to the multicolored folders. "See. I use color in my daily life, too."

"I noticed that." Nell gave him a smile. "It's useful, isn't it?"

"It is to me. Do you mind if I ask? What's it like to be able to see so many colors in the world?"

"I'm not sure how to answer that. I've never seen the world the way most other people do, but from talking to my sister and my parents and our friends, I think the way I see things is richly beautiful, nuanced, wild. The way most people see colors seems to me to be more calm and orderly while still being beautiful. There are times when what I see is overwhelming, like when I go into a grocery store ... there are so many things going on with products stacked tightly together. The colors can be clashing with each other because there are too many shades competing with the others. Product designers choose several colors for their package designs and even though it looks attractive to most people, to me the multiple shades clash and the presentation looks way too busy and loud and makes me want to avoid the product." Nell shrugged.

"I bet it can be exhausting," the chief said.

"It can. My eyes get tired. My head gets tired. I need a calming space with few colors. The wall color in here is calming and easy on my eyes." She glanced around at the mess and gave the chief a little smile. "The clutter ... well, not so much."

"Hey," Chief Lambert said. "This is a very important mess."

Nell explained more about how the world looked to her and then the conversation turned to Pepper Forrest's case.

"Have you seen colors on any other people?" the chief asked.

"I saw colors on the witnesses when I spoke with them. The colors came from the emotions evoked from recalling the details of what they'd seen when Pepper was hit by the car. Anger, disbelief, sadness, horror. They couldn't believe someone could hit a person with a car and take off from the scene without stopping to see if they could help the victim. The musician, Mick Jones, he thinks it was a deliberate act on the part of the driver. He strongly believes it was intentional."

The chief nodded in agreement. "He said as much to us when he was interviewed right after the accident. He's perceptive. We're looking into where the medical researcher, Atkins Murray, was during the timeframe when Pepper was hit. So far, no luck."

"Atkins must think he's a suspect," Nell said.

"I'm not sure if he does or not. We spoke with

quite a few employees at the medical center. Dr. Murray might think we talked to him as part of a general gathering of information. Our interest is due to him having dated Dr. Forrest and being sullen about the breakup, and that you saw him covered in red when you spoke with him."

"I'm sorry my new skill isn't that helpful," Nell said.

Chief Lambert moved his hand around in the air. "Don't say that. Your skill is very new. You need to learn about it. My hope is that someday, when it's more fully developed, it might become a valuable asset to the department. Unusual skills have helped many police investigations. I don't dismiss anyone's skills. To me, it's nothing more than a heightened sensory ability. I don't think humans tap into anywhere near what is possible for them to do or achieve. Most of us hold ourselves back. We don't push. We don't believe certain things are possible. And then we miss opportunities."

"When I'm talking to you, I feel almost normal." The corners of Nell's mouth turned up and the chief let out a hoot of laughter.

"None of us are normal, Nell. Everyone has their own special quirks and oddities. It gives life its spice. How awful it would be if we were all the same."

A knock on the door caused Nell and Chief Lambert to turn to the sound.

"Come on in," the chief said and an officer came into the office carrying a plastic bag with some documents inside.

"Here's what you asked for," the officer held out the bag.

The chief thanked the man and when he had gone, Lambert placed the item on the table. He went to his desk and returned to Nell with a pair of surgical gloves.

"You'll need to wear these while you're handling the papers. Put on the gloves before you remove the documents," the chief instructed. "Don't take them off until you return the papers to the bag and seal it."

Nell nodded and pulled on the gloves.

"I'm going to let you have the room to yourself. I'll be in the conference room next door doing some paperwork. Come by when you're done and leave the evidence bag with me."

"Okay," Nell said.

After the chief picked up a few folders and his laptop and left the room, Nell looked down at the bag with apprehension. A nervous wave of heat started in her chest and made its way up to her cheeks. She didn't know why looking over some papers should make her feel so anxious.

When she removed the four-page lease agreement from the bag, she spread the documents onto the table and let her eyes roam over the pages, and then she started to read.

The words were a mix of legalese and common directions and statements about the lessee's responsibilities and expectations. Scrawled initials had been placed at regular intervals on sections of the documents by the person who rented the car. On the last page, at the bottom, was the person's signature written in green ink.

Justin Carr.

Nell's cheeks reddened with anger and her heartbeat increased. *Liar. Murderer.*

She touched her gloved index finger to the signature.

Without warning, the green letters flared red with such intensity in Nell's vision that she yanked her finger away from the document.

The letters slowly settled back to their original shade.

Staring at the signature, Nell swallowed hard and gingerly lifted her hand to place her finger back onto the killer's autograph. This time the letters shimmered and changed color less dramatically, but soon they were flaring red, almost lifting from the page like burning flames.

Uneasily, Nell forced herself to keep her finger against the paper, and then she closed her eyes trying to pick up anything she could from the dried ink on the page about the person who placed it there.

Her body began to fill with a sense of rage ... with a feeling of having been wronged ... a perception of a boiling, uncontrollable need for revenge.

Nell's eyes popped open as she pulled her shaking finger from the lease. Her eyes stared at the squiggly green ink thinking about the furious, blazing energy the killer had transferred to the page in front of her. An energy so strong, the sensation still lingered on the document sapping away Nell's own vitality.

Her muscles ached and she had the fleeting idea to curl up on the floor and fall asleep. Nell stood, shaking herself and wanting nothing more than to rush away from the toxic emotions she'd felt from the signature.

Whoever signed the lease was consumed with vengeance.

Standing still and looking down at the rental car

agreement, she wondered what could cause such feelings. What could have happened to make the driver of the car turn to murder? What could the driver have believed about Pepper where the only solution was to kill her?

An icy chill ran down her back.

Nell shoved the lease back into the evidence bag before tugging off the surgical gloves and tossing them into the trash basket near the chief's desk. She took the bag and hurried out of the office to the conference room.

The door was open and Chief Lambert sat at the long table working at his laptop. Nell appeared in the room with such suddenness that the man looked up quickly from his work.

"What's wrong? What happened?"

Nell sank into the chair beside him, and pushing her auburn hair behind her ears and leaning her head onto her hand, she told what she saw and felt while examining the lease agreement.

Chief Lambert tried to keep his expression even, but his eyebrows rose up his forehead as Nell talked.

"Well. That's amazing," he said when she'd finished reporting what had happened.

"It wasn't any help though. It didn't reveal anything about the killer ... except that he had to settle a score, he had to exact revenge. It was his mission and he wouldn't stop until he punished whoever he believed to have wronged him."

"It tells us more than we knew before you looked at the rental paperwork," Chief Lambert told her. "Someone was out for revenge. Some slight or harm done had to be punished."

"It sort of fits with David Belk, doesn't it?" Nell suggested. "He is enraged that Pepper gave him the bad grade. He blames her for ruining his chances of getting the jobs he wanted. To his way of thinking, Pepper ruined his life."

The chief gave a nod. "It also could fit in with Dr. Atkins Murray. He hasn't come right out and stated it, but I bet he feels Pepper destroyed his chance at love and a permanent relationship. And from what you've told me, he harbored feelings of resentment towards Pepper. Maybe he's careful not to verbalize any stronger feelings of anger he had for Pepper."

Nell looked down at the table, shaken by the experience with the car lease. "There's something else that bothers me about all this." She paused before going on. "Is there anyone else the killer thinks he has to snuff out? Is there someone else in danger? Or has the mission been completed with Pepper's death?"

21

The three small seascape paintings were finished, carefully wrapped, and ready for delivery to William at The Sandy Rose. Nell was relieved to have completed the commissioned work on time and she carried the paintings inside to the inn.

She was surprised to see William standing in the foyer behind the check-in desk looking frazzled. Two couples were waiting for their keys, but the rooms were still being cleaned. Another couple was ready to check out and looked impatient about having to wait.

An older woman hurried up to William brushing aside a man and woman. "The faucet in the bathtub won't turn off. It's going to overflow."

Nell placed the paintings in William's office and came back out front to hear what the woman had just reported.

"I used the walkie-talkie to contact Bobby, but he isn't answering," William told Nell.

"Shall I go upstairs and see if I can turn off the faucet?"

"Would you?" William looked at the young woman with desperation. "What a day."

In a few minutes, Nell was back downstairs. "I got a bucket from the housekeeper and used it to drain some of the water out of the tub. I couldn't turn off the faucet. Did Bobby respond to your call?"

William shook his head. "I called his phone, too, and he still doesn't answer. Will you run down to the workshop and his cottage and see if he's there? As soon as I'm done here, I'll go up and start bailing out the bathtub."

"What about a turnoff in the basement?" Nell asked.

"It's broken. Bobby hasn't fixed it. I'm going to call a plumber to do it. Bobby gave his notice and is leaving in two weeks. I'm scrambling to find someone to take his place."

"He's leaving? Where is he going?" Nell asked.

"He's moving back to the West Coast."

"Mr. Mathers, would you check us out, please," a woman insisted.

"I'll go see if I can find him." Nell darted from the inn and jogged down the pathway that led to Bobby's cottage. When she reached the house, she knocked on the front door, but no one answered so she headed over to the workshop building.

The door to the shop was open. "Bobby?" Nell called and stepped inside.

Bobby wasn't in the workshop and Nell noticed that a good amount of the man's tools and many of his woodworking products had already been moved out of the space.

The handyman's desk was in a corner of the room near the door. Nell saw a pad of paper and a wooden pen crafted by the handyman, so she went over and wrote a short note telling Bobby about the urgent bathtub problem.

The desk drawer was partially open and Nell couldn't help seeing a small framed photo of Bobby and a woman at a beach, embracing one another and smiling out from the picture. The two of them looked happy and carefree.

Nell heard the scuff of a work boot at the door's threshold and she looked up to see Bobby coming into the workshop carrying some empty clay flowerpots.

He stared at Nell. "What are you doing?" The color pink started to shade the man from his feet to his head, and then the color changed from pink to a deep, dark red.

"Nothing." Nell stammered feeling like she'd been caught doing something wrong. "I was looking for you. I left a note. A bathtub is overflowing at the inn. William couldn't contact you. He needs you right away."

Bobby glanced at the open desk drawer and the colors he reflected began to change from red to green to orange, and back to red.

Feeling like she'd invaded the handyman's space, Nell moved towards the door. "William was becoming desperate. I offered to come find you. I need to get back to my store. See you later. Good luck with the tub."

SITTING in the studio in the backroom of the shop, Nell and Violet sipped iced teas while Nell told her sister what had happened at the inn when she'd dropped off the artwork. Iris rested in her dog bed in the corner of the room, but she had her eyes open and her ears twitched every now and then as if she was listening to the conversation.

"Bobby's moving away?" Violet asked.

"That's what William said. It must be a sudden decision because William is desperate to find someone to take Bobby's place before he leaves."

"Remember when we were in the garage getting ready for our bike ride and Bobby came in to apologize for being a little rude when you tried to talk to him?" Violet asked.

Nell nodded.

"He said he had some things on his mind," Violet recalled. "This move must have been what he was debating about."

"You must be right. I wonder why he wants to move out west."

"Maybe he's looking for a place with a milder winter. I wouldn't blame him one bit. A move to a warmer climate sounds pretty good when it's winter."

Nell told her sister how uncomfortable she felt when Bobby came into the workshop. "I felt like I had invaded his space. He seemed wary of me, like I'd been spying on him. I almost felt guilty."

"You were looking for him. The door was open. It was a plumbing emergency."

"He'd left the desk drawer open," Nell said. "I saw a photo of him with a woman tucked away in the drawer. He looked at me like I had opened all the drawers and was snooping around."

"Gosh, you'd never do that," Violet said.

"I know that and you know that, but Bobby doesn't know me and he doesn't know I'd never go through someone's things."

"He got angry, huh? You picked up on his emotions?"

"I did. He wasn't pleased about me being near his desk," Nell said. "I saw red all over him. Orange, too. And green."

"What does green represent?" Violet asked.

"It was really dark green, almost black."

"What does it mean?"

Nell lifted her phone and checked her notes for the list of colors and their meanings that she'd saved. "Black can mean a bunch of things from life, to mystery, to death. Green can represent envy, rebirth, wisdom." Shaking her head, she said, "I don't have a clue what a greenish-black color could mean."

"You need to talk to someone who can see what you can see," Violet suggested.

"Yeah." Nell rested her chin in her hand and rolled her eyes. "Good luck finding that person. I think I'm on my own here."

Violet said, "I can't see the colors, but I can offer you support and be a sounding-board for you. We can put our heads together. I know I'm not that much help, but you're never completely on your own."

Nell gave her sister a soft smile and a hug. "I know that, and I'm not sure what I'd do without you."

Iris yipped from her place on her dog bed and wagged her tail.

"I don't know what I'd do without you either." Violet teased, "You sure keep life interesting."

"Sometimes, too interesting." Nell shook her head. "I need to apologize to Bobby next time he's here working on the deck for barging into his work space without permission."

"You think that's necessary?"

"I do. We wouldn't like it if someone came back here if we weren't around."

"That's true," Violet agreed. "You're right. I think Bobby would appreciate the apology."

Nell looked out the window and out to the ocean way off in the distance. "Ever since I got home from the inn, something's been picking at me about that car rental agreement I looked at."

"Really? What is it that's bothering you?"

"That's just it. I don't know." Nell's mind kept returning to the document. Images of the four-page lease had been popping into her mind making her feel uneasy and anxious.

"It might be because you know the person who signed it is a killer," Violet said with disgust in her voice. "You saw his signature. You know he leased the car for one purpose. To run down Pepper Forrest."

"It's a sickening thought," Nell said. "The killer held that document right in his hands. If only the police could retrieve DNA from the paper."

Violet sat up. "Did they try to get fingerprints from it?"

"There was nothing viable." Nell sighed. "The person who signed that paper was careful about that."

"What about the pen he used? Did he leave any fingerprints on that?"

Nell said, "The clerk at the rental company thought the guy used his own pen, and even if he didn't, so many other people would have used the same pen that there would be no way to isolate one print from another."

Violet groaned. "The killer was smart. He used a disguise, he wore sunglasses and a wig. The security camera's film is fuzzy. Things were really stacked in his favor."

"There has to be something," Nell said almost in a whisper. "There has to be one little thing that will tip the scales in favor of figuring this out. All we need is that one little thing."

22

N ell couldn't shake the feeling that she was missing something and she'd been staring at her laptop screen for two hours since Violet and Iris had gone into the main part of the house to head to bed. She'd been searching for information about Pepper Forrest's background and so far had come up empty.

Nell found a minor reference of Pepper teaching at the high school in California and the more recent information about her being on staff at the university, but that was mostly it. Despite searching for news articles reporting the accident that killed her husband, Nell was striking out.

On impulse, she picked up her phone and sent off a text. Because it was so late, she didn't expect a reply until morning, so she shut down the laptop with a yawn, and dragged herself to bed.

ON SUNDAY MORNING, Nell was up with the sun and because the shop wouldn't open until noon, Violet went out for a long run.

Nell could hear Bobby outside sawing boards and pounding on the deck, and she thought he must want to get the work done as soon as possible since he was planning his move in a couple of weeks. Deciding to go out to talk to him, she called to Iris to come with her.

"Hey," Nell called to Bobby. "How are things going?"

Bobby put down his hammer. "Fine."

"Did you get the inn's bathtub water problem taken care of?" she asked trying to be friendly.

"Yeah. I did." Bobby kicked at a stray nail on the deck. His manner was awkward and strained and he made Nell feel uncomfortable.

John and Ida were having coffee on their porch and they waved warmly to their young neighbor. Iris spotted the couple, wagged her tail, and trotted across the lawn to go and sit with them.

"William told me you're moving away," Nell said. "What made you decide to leave?"

Bobby gave a shrug. "It's time for a change."

"Are you moving to California?"

"Haven't decided yet. Maybe Oregon."

"Will you able to finish the deck before you leave?"

"It'll get done. Don't worry about it."

Nell didn't care for Bobby's sullen attitude and didn't think he should be acting so rude to her just because she'd gone into his workshop when he wasn't there, but she decided she should respect his feelings. "Listen, I'm sorry about going into the workshop when you weren't there. I should have waited for you to come back. I shouldn't have gone inside without permission."

Bobby glared at Nell and used a sarcastic tone when he asked, "Did you find what you were looking for?"

"I was looking for you," Nell said defensively.

Red color began to flare and pulse all over Bobby's frame, and Nell took a step back from him.

"I wasn't spying on you. William needed you. He needed you right away. I left you a note."

Bobby balled his hand into a fist. "You shouldn't go snooping around. I don't appreciate it."

"I wasn't snooping." Nell wheeled around and strode away to go back inside the house, her head pounding with anger. She couldn't believe Bobby's reaction. She'd apologized to him. He didn't accept it. Nell wished the man would hurry up and finish the deck so she wouldn't have to see him ever again.

Nell's poor mood eased somewhat after making an omelette for breakfast and drinking a cup of tea, and while sitting at the kitchen table with her laptop, she heard her phone buzz and saw an incoming text from Chief Lambert.

The chief answered the questions she'd asked in her text from the previous night.

Pepper's real name was Penelope, her surname prior to marriage was Forrest, her husband's name was Justin Randolph. It was never clear if Pepper changed her last name after marriage, kept her maiden name, or changed it to Randolph briefly and then changed it back to Forrest. The chief suggested that when doing a search on Pepper, Nell should try using both of the last names. Chief Lambert also gave her the date of Pepper and Justin's marriage.

After trying different combinations of names in a search, Nell finally found the articles she'd hoped for.

This time an obituary for Justin Randolph came

up on the screen as well as a news story about the man's fatal accident.

The article reported that Justin Randolph died when his car crashed through a small barrier on the California coast road and plummeted off the cliffs to the rocks below, killing him instantly. He left a wife of eight months, Penelope Forrest, a local high school teacher. The cause of the accident was still being investigated, but initial reports pointed to a faulty brake line.

When Nell sat up straight and blinked, her heart began to race. *A faulty brake line?*

She scanned the news reports for the name of the reporter.

Bradley Pointer.

Nell did a search for the man and discovered he was still working for the same news service, and more importantly she found his email address. After composing an email to Bradley Pointer, Nell hoped he'd be up early and at his laptop despite the time difference between the coasts.

The next thing she wanted to find was an article about the car accident Pepper and her fiancé had been involved in that required months of recovery for both of them. Searching and scrolling for several minutes, this time with the correct names, she discovered the article she'd been hunting for.

Penelope Forrest, 22, and her fiancé, Justin Randolph, 25, were seriously injured in a two-vehicle accident. Mr. Randolph missed a stop sign and drove through an intersection hitting a car occupied by a couple in their mid-twenties. Melinda Prince was pronounced dead at the scene. Her husband, J.R. Prince, was hospitalized with serious head injuries.

Nell leaned back and took in a long breath. The woman died. How devastating. What a terrible accident to be involved in.

When she heard a ding from her inbox, Nell was thrilled to see a response from Bradley Pointer. He remembered the accident of over ten years ago that killed Pepper's husband and he'd pulled up his notes on it. Justin was driving an old car and it was totaled in the crash off the cliffs. The brake line was worn through, but the investigators couldn't be sure if the line was cut due to age, from the crash, or from someone tampering with it.

Justin's wife, Pepper Forrest, worried the accident might be the result of foul play because although the car was old, Justin kept everything in good working order. Ms. Forrest was devastated by the loss of her husband and she decided to give notice at her teaching job and move to the East Coast.

As Nell stared at the words in the email, a vague anxiety pulsed through her veins. What am I missing? Closing her eyes and leaning her forehead into her hands, she sat quietly at the table thinking through everything she knew. The details swirled in her head like a whirlwind and she tried to grasp at the different strands to make sense of them.

Colors began to flash in her mind. Red, black, orange, green. Over and over. Faster and faster until she began to feel ill.

Nell's eyes popped open.

Green. Green.

Nell tapped away at her laptop while spots of perspiration beaded up on her forehead.

When the photo in the obituary she was looking for showed on the screen, Nell gasped and grasped the edge of the table.

The photograph of Melinda Prince, the woman who died in the car crash with Pepper and her fiancé, looked very much like the woman standing in the photo next to Bobby that Nell saw in the desk drawer in the workshop on the inn's grounds.

Jumping to her feet, she nearly knocked over her chair as she darted into the large pantry off the kitchen where she and Violet kept a small file cabinet for their personal papers and receipts. Yanking open the file drawers, Nell searched for the manila folder she was looking for and when she found it, she opened it and stared at the contract.

Her heart sank into her stomach and her breathing came hard and shallow.

Bobby's signature on the deck contract was in green ink.

The rental car contract had been signed with green ink.

The rental car clerk was fairly certain the man who leased the vehicle had used his own pen.

Nell had watched Bobby sign the contract with one of his handmade pens ... a pen with green ink.

Lifting the contract for the deck repair closer to her eyes, she tried to make out the green ink scrawl of Bobby's signature. *What is his last name? How do we not know his last name? Does this say Prince?* Nell groaned. *Would he write his real name on the contract?*

Nell rushed to the door of the pantry to return to the kitchen. She wanted to call Violet.

Stepping out of the pantry, Nell stopped dead.

Bobby was standing in the kitchen.

23

———

Nell's throat was so tight she could barely breath. Bobby stood on the other side of the kitchen by the door. His face was moist with sweat and a few strands of his hair stuck to his forehead. His expression was blank.

"You need something?" Nell squeezed the words out.

Bobby didn't say anything, he just held her eyes with his.

Although the urge to run pulsed in Nell's head, she knew it was a stupid idea. She couldn't get far without Bobby being right at her heels. Darting away would only enrage him. No. It would be better to stay in the kitchen close to the door to the outside. Maybe if she got him talking, she could buy time until Violet returned home. Maybe she'd see them in the kitchen and would call for help.

Nell's heart sank thinking about Violet walking into danger. She had to get Bobby out of the house. She had to keep Violet safe.

"Do you need something?" Nell asked again trying to keep the fear out of her voice.

"Why are you so interested in Pepper Forrest?" Bobby's upper lip twitched.

"What do you mean?" Nell pretended not to know what he was talking about.

Bobby's voice sounded impatient. "Why are you going around town asking so many questions about her?"

"Am I?"

"Are you working with the police?" Bobby demanded.

"The police? I'm an artist. What use would the police have for me?"

"You tell me." Bobby took a step towards the young woman.

Nell turned the tables on the handyman by questioning him. "Why are you asking me these things? Why are you in my kitchen asking me foolish questions? What are you trying to get me mixed up in?"

Bobby looked taken aback for a second. "Why were you snooping around my desk?"

"I told you. William needed your help. I left a note for you so you'd go to the inn to help. The desk drawer was open. I didn't open it." Everything she said was the truth. The drawer *was* open. She *hadn't* been spying on Bobby. Nell decided to play-up being wrongly accused. "How dare you accuse me of snooping."

Nell moved her feet a few inches forward wanting to get as close to the door as possible without triggering the man to attack. She said, "You're acting like you have something to hide. Why don't you go back and work on the deck and I'll forget you came into my home uninvited?"

"Why did you go to the car rental place with that cop?" Bobby's eyes had darkened.

You followed me, Nell thought, her blood starting to boil. "Were you following me? Why were you? That *cop* is dating my best friend. We socialize. We do things together. He wants to rent a car for a trip," she lied. "I went with him to get the information."

When Bobby leaned forward, his face was tight ... it looked mean. "That's not what the counter clerk told me. He told me you were asking questions about the guy who rented the car that hit that professor."

Nell's stomach turned to ice, but she managed to keep her anger audible in her voice. "I'm nosy. So what?"

"What's the purpose of your nosiness?" Bobby dared her to explain.

"That woman was in our shop moments before she got hit. Violet and I wonder what happened."

"She got run over. That's what happened." Bobby moved slightly and Nell spotted the hammer he held in his hand. Her vision dimmed a little from the terror racing through her veins. She would have to face the situation head-on. It was her only chance.

"Why don't we go into the shop?" Bobby suggested.

"Why?" Nell asked.

Nell knew he wanted to get her away from the door and the windows. Then he would attack.

"I want to look around," Bobby told her.

"Why are you suddenly moving away from Massachusetts?" Nell asked, trying to distract him.

Bobby narrowed his eyes. "Because." The word came out like a hiss.

Nell looked for something close by that she could use to strike Bobby with. She spotted the frying pan on the cooled burner, and as she took a step closer to the stove, through the open kitchen window she heard the *click-click-click* of a bike.

Returning from her early morning ride, Violet walked her bicycle towards the garage and when she glanced into the house through the window, Nell met her eyes with an expression of dread and gave a tiny shake of her head.

Bobby hadn't noticed the slight exchange between Nell and her sister. The man's chest was rapidly rising and falling. He clenched and unclenched his free hand. Nell knew he was getting ready to strike.

"What's your last name?" Nell asked the man. "I've never heard it."

"The last name I was born with? Or the one I changed it to?" The bright red color covering Bobby sparked and flared.

"Melinda died in an accident, didn't she?" Nell asked, referring to his late wife. "It seems you blamed Pepper Forrest and her then-fiancé for your wife's death."

Bobby's body shook. His eyes nearly popped from their sockets. "They killed her," he shrieked. "So I killed them."

"And now because of an accident, you're a

murderer." Nell watched the man's face. She was ready.

When Bobby lunged, Nell grabbed the cast iron frying pan from the stovetop and bashed him in the face just as Violet, swinging a crowbar she'd taken from Bobby's truck, crashed into the kitchen. The dog flew past Violet to get to the man who had fallen to his knees.

Then the two-person backup charged through the door behind Violet and the dog. Ida held a baseball bat at her shoulder and John wielded a metal rake, and they weren't afraid to use them.

Bobby slumped to the floor, his nose spouting blood.

"We called the police," Ida said. "They'll be here soon."

"You okay, sis?" Violet put her arm around her sister's shoulders.

"Just fine. Now that all of you are here." Nell sank into one of the kitchen chairs as Violet, Iris, John, and Ida stood ready to handle Bobby Prince should he make the wrong decision to move.

24

"Things just started to click, and then the pieces fell into place," Nell told Chief Lambert. They sat in the police chief's office with the door closed. "I finally found some articles I was looking for on the accident Pepper and her fiancé were in and a story about the crash that killed her husband, Justin. When I read someone died from the collision with Justin and Pepper's car, and that the woman's husband survived with head injuries, I became very uneasy, but didn't understand why."

"Then you remembered the friend telling you Pepper received a threatening note that contributed to her decision to leave California?" the chief asked.

"The little details began to add up," Nell said. "I didn't understand the whole picture at that point, but my subconscious must have been on the right path. I found the obituary picture of Melinda Prince and she looked a great deal like the woman in the photo I saw in Bobby's desk. The green ink signature on the rental car agreement kept coming into my mind. The clerk at the rental place thought the man used his own pen to sign the contract. That's when I recalled that when Bobby signed the deck restoration contract, his pen produced green ink."

"You found the contract in the file cabinet," the chief stated. "You knew it had to be Bobby who killed Pepper Forrest. And you were right." The chief rubbed at the back of his neck. "As it turns out, Bobby changed his last name from Prince to Price. He stopped using J. R. and used only Bobby as his first name. He also kept plenty of notebooks over the years, filling them with angry rants against Pepper and Justin, love letters to his late wife, complaints about his life. Over the years, Bobby kept tabs on Pepper. He used the internet to find out where she was and what she was doing. Bobby's wife had been a Ph.D. student at the time of her death. It seems he resented Pepper for obtaining her Ph.D. when his wife never got to achieve that goal for herself."

Nell's eyes were wide with disbelief that Bobby held a murderous grudge for so long.

The chief continued, "Bobby decided to act against Pepper when he discovered she'd secured a position as a professor at Fuller University in Boston. He looked for work in the Boston area, found the job at The Sandy Rose, and started working there last January. The job was flexible and gave him free lodging. He used his days off to follow Pepper in Boston and learn her routines. He detailed all of this in his journals. His plan was to kill Pepper by running her down with a car. As fate or coincidence would have it, Pepper came to Bluewater Cove to attend a symposium and she booked lodging at The Sandy Rose. Bobby saw her at the inn and couldn't believe his luck. He delighted in slipping a note under Pepper's door telling her to watch her back. He wanted to frighten her in order to make her miserable. He rented a car, and completed his mission." Chief Lambert's eyes were heavy with sadness.

"All of this was in Bobby's notebooks?" Nell asked.

"Yes, and plenty more," the chief said. "Bobby's notes tell us he tampered with the brake line on Justin's car and caused the crash that killed him. It took Bobby years to plot and carry out Pepper's murder, but he finally achieved his goal of taking the lives of the two people he blamed for his wife's death."

"I guess Bobby believes in the saying, an eye for an eye," Nell said sadly. "I wonder if Pepper thought Bobby Prince was responsible for both her husband's crash and the threatening note she received?"

"She may have suspected Bobby, but the police in her California hometown have no record that Pepper reported her concerns to them," Chief Lambert said. "She may have talked to them about it, but it isn't on record."

"When Bobby lived in California, he went by J.R?" Nell asked.

"His legal name is Jason Robert Prince. He used J.R. until he found out where Pepper was living and followed her to the Boston area ... then he started going by Bobby *Price*. Before he left California, he arranged to have false IDs created and obtained a credit card with the name Justin Carr on it. Bobby took the job at The Sandy Rose because it was part-time at first, was close to the city, and it gave him time to scout out Pepper's daily movements. He initially thought of attacking her in the city, but decided to wait until she was in a less crowded location. We'll never really know for sure what Pepper knew or what her plans were."

"Why didn't she just go to the police with her concerns?" Nell sighed. "She shouldn't have tried to do things on her own. If she spoke to the police about her worries, maybe she'd still be alive."

"Unfortunately, there would be little the police could do if Pepper went to them only with concerns," Chief Lambert said as he cocked his head to the side. "You said you saw colors in your mind when you were thinking over the details of the case. The flashing colors made you think of the green ink? That's what made you remember Bobby's pen had green ink?"

Nell nodded. "I closed my eyes for a minute and then the colors began to flash. Green became the dominant color, and then I realized why. Bobby signed the deck contract with his own pen. It had green ink. The car rental contract was signed in green ink, too."

"Fascinating," the chief said. "There was something else in Bobby's notes. He heard you and The Sandy Roses's owner discussing Pepper right after she died. He was suspicious of you so he made a late-night visit to your house to see where you lived."

Nell's eyes went wide. "My neighbor and I

thought we saw someone in the shadows snooping around near the house one night."

"You were right," the chief said. "I want to thank you for your help with this case. Would you be interested in working with us again should the need arise? I think you're only tapping the surface of what you'll be able to do."

A shiver ran down Nell's back. She never again wanted to be involved with a police case, and she almost declined the chief's request to work with them in the future ... and then she realized that her strange skill of seeing colors on and around people could be used for good ... it could be used to help the good guys win.

Nell took in a long breath. "If you need me again, you know where to find me."

A wide smile brightened Chief Lambert's face.

UNDER THE SPARKLING STARS, Ida, John, Nell, and Violet sat around the circular table on the deck enjoying a meal of spaghetti and meatballs with green salads.

"I hope that monster did enough work on this

deck so it won't give way while we're out here," John said.

"I jumped up and down on it before you came over," Nell smiled. "I didn't fall through."

"You don't weigh as much as all of us out here at the same time," John said.

"Well, if it collapses, at least we'll all go down together." Violet passed the bowl of parmesan cheese to the older man.

"That's not that comforting." John sprinkled some cheese over the pasta.

"If it's any consolation, it's not that far to fall," Nell offered.

"Great." John chuckled. "Just don't forget to help me up."

Ida shook her head. "We'll leave you to fend for yourself."

"I won't leave you," Nell promised. "I owe you. All of you. I'll never forget how you came to my aid, armed and ready to do damage."

"You don't owe us anything, my dear," John told her. "We take care of each other. You'd do the same for us."

Iris woofed from her resting spot on the deck.

"I've never been so frightened in all my life." Nell wiped at her eyes.

With a smile, Violet reached over to her sister. "You did a good job of hitting him with that frying pan. I bet you could have handled him all by yourself."

"I'm glad I didn't have to try."

"Your skills saved the day," Ida told Nell. "It was such a small detail. If you didn't think of the green ink, Bobby Prince, or whatever name he uses, would have gotten away with the murders of those two people."

"The police would have figured it out eventually," Nell said.

Ida raised an eyebrow and gave her a look of disbelief. "No, they wouldn't have."

The front doorbell rang and Nell rose to go see who it was. "Who would be here at this time of night?"

After looking through the peephole, Nell opened the door wide and saw the huge bouquet of flowers in the man's hands. "Rob. What are you doing here?"

"I know I texted you a bunch over the past couple of days, but I wanted to see with my own eyes that you were okay. I was worried." With a smile, Rob handed her the bouquet. "These are for you. You *are* okay, right?"

"I'm fine. I'm good." Nell sniffed the beautiful white flowers. "Thank you for these, and for the texts, too. I appreciated them."

"I picked all white flowers because I know you find that color calming. I thought you might need some calm after what you went through." Rob shifted his feet on the front step.

"You're very thoughtful." When Nell looked into Rob's eyes, she was surprised by the warm feeling that spread through her chest.

"Well, I just wanted to check on you. Sorry I didn't call first. It was a spur of the moment thing. I'm really glad you're okay. Why don't you come to the lab next week? We can run together if you're up for it." Rob started to turn away.

"Wait. Stay. John and Ida are here having dinner with me and Violet out on the deck. Have you eaten? Come join us."

"Oh, no. I don't want to interrupt."

"You're not interrupting."

Rob hesitated. "Are you sure?"

"I'm positive." When Nell reached for his hand to encourage him to come inside, unexpected little sparks seemed to jump between them causing her heart to flutter. "I'm glad you're here."

"I'm glad I'm here, too." Rob's smile melted Nell's heart ... and the two friends headed out to the deck to join the others.

THANK YOU FOR READING!

Books by J.A. WHITING can be found here:
www.amazon.com/author/jawhiting

To hear about new books and book sales, please sign
up for my mailing list at:
www.jawhitingbooks.com

Your email will never be sold, shared, or spammed.

If you enjoyed the book, please consider leaving a
review. A few words are all that's needed. It would be
very much appreciated.

BOOKS/SERIES BY J. A. WHITING

CLAIRE ROLLINS COZY MYSTERIES

LIN COFFIN COZY MYSTERIES

PAXTON PARK COZY MYSTERIES

SWEET COVE COZY MYSTERIES

OLIVIA MILLER MYSTERIES (not cozy)

SEEING COLORS MYSTERIES

ABOUT THE AUTHOR

J.A. Whiting lives with her family in New England. Whiting loves reading and writing mystery stories.

Visit me at:

http://www.jawhitingbooks.com/
www.facebook.com/jawhitingauthor
www.bookbub.com/authors/j-a-whiting

34452840R00151

Made in the USA
Lexington, KY
24 March 2019